Penguin Books
The Innocent Libertine

Colette, the creator of Claudine, Chéri and Gigi, and one
of France's outstanding writers, had a long, varied and
active life. She was born in Burgundy in 1873, into a home
overflowing with dogs, cats and children, and educated
at the local village school. At the age of twenty she was
brought to Paris by her first husband, the notorious
Henry Gauthiers-Villars (Willy), writer and critic. By
dint of locking her in her room, Willy forced Colette to
write her first novels (the Claudine sequence), which he
published under his name. They were an instant success.
But their marriage (chronicled in *Mes Apprentissages*)
was never happy and Colette left him in 1906. She spent the
next six years on the stage – an experience, like that of
her country childhood, which would provide many of the
themes for her work. She remarried (*Julie de Carneilhan*
'is as close a reckoning with the elements of her second
marriage as she ever allowed herself'), later divorcing her
second husband, by whom she had a daughter. In 1935 she
married Maurice Goudeket, with whom she lived until
her death in 1954.

With the publication of *Chéri* (1920), Colette's place as
one of France's prose masters became assured. Although
she became increasingly crippled with arthritis, she
never lost her intense preoccupation with everything
around her. 'I cannot interest myself in anything that is
not life,' she said; and, to a young writer, 'Look for a long
time at what pleases you, and longer still at what pains
you'. Her rich and supple prose, with its sensuous detail
and sharp psychological insights, illustrates that
personal philosophy.

Her writings run to fifteen volumes: novels, portraits,
essays, *chroniques* and a large body of autobiographical
prose. She was the first woman President of the Académie
Goncourt, and when she died was given a state funeral
and buried in Père-Lachaise cemetery in Paris.

Colette

The Innocent Libertine

Translated from the French by
Antonia White

Penguin Books
in association with Martin Secker & Warburg Ltd

Penguin Books Ltd, Harmondsworth,
Middlesex, England
Penguin Books, 625 Madison Avenue,
New York, New York 10022, U.S.A.
Penguin Books Canada Ltd, 2801 John Street,
Markham, Ontario, Canada L3R 1B4
Penguin Books Australia Ltd, Ringwood,
Victoria, Australia
Penguin Books (N.Z.) Ltd 182–190 Wairau Road,
Auckland 10, New Zealand

This translation first published by Martin Secker &
Warburg 1968
Published in Penguin Books 1972
Reprinted 1980

The Innocent Libertine was first published in two volumes,
Minne and *Les Égarements de Minne*, by Paul Ollendorff
Library in 1904 and 1905 with 'Mr Willy' as the author.
It was first published in one volume as *L'Ingénue Libertine*
with 'Colette Willy' as author in 1909. First published
in the definitive French edition by Albin Michel in 1948.

Set, printed and bound in Great Britain by
Cox & Wyman Ltd, Reading
Set in Intertype Baskerville

Preface

When I wrote *Minne,* I intended to write only a long short story, in the hope that I could sign it with my own name. It was necessary therefore, since any work of the dimensions of a novel was bound to be appropriated by covetous hands, that my story should be quite short. It was; but not for long. Its success proved fatal to it. I heard words of praise from a husband's mouth; I also heard other words, too strong for me to quote in this preface. I had to pad out *Minne* somewhat.

Let those who have never longed for peace as the greatest of all goods throw the first stone at me: I had to go on and write *Les Égarements de Minne,* which I have never considered a good novel.

Was it better when later, after it had become my property again, I abridged it and revised it and welded it on to *Minne* to make a single book under the title *L'Ingénue Libertine*? I should be only too glad to think so but I fear that this definitive edition itself fails to convince me of this or to reconcile me completely to the first aspects of my career as a novelist.

COLETTE

Part One

'Minne? ... Minne darling, surely you've finished that essay! Minne, you'll ruin your eyes!'

Minne gave an impatient mumble. She had already replied: 'Yes, Mamma' three times to Mamma who was embroidering behind the back of the big armchair.

Minne nibbled her ivory pen-holder. Her head was bent so low over her exercise book that nothing could be seen but the silver of her fair hair and the tip of a delicate nose between two drooping ringlets.

The fire muttered softly, the oil-lamp counted the seconds drop by drop, Mamma sighed. At every stitch on the canvas she was embroidering – a big collar for Minne – her needle made a little pecking noise. Outside, the plane-trees of the Boulevard Berthier dripped with rain and the trams of the outer boulevards that followed the line of the old fortifications grated musically on their rails.

Mamma cut the thread of her embroidery. At the clink of the little scissors, Minne's delicate nose went up, the silver hair was flung back and two beautiful dark eyes appeared, alertly on the watch. It was only a false alarm. Mamma was tranquilly threading another needle and Minne could bend down again over the open newspaper, half concealed under her history exercise-book. Slowly and carefully she read the column headed *Paris at Night*:

Do our municipal authorities even realize that certain quarters of Paris, in particular the outer boulevards, are as dangerous for anyone who ventures there on foot as the Prairie is for the white traveller? Our modern apaches give full rein to their natural savagery there; not a night passes without one or more corpses being picked up in the vicinity.

Let us thank Heaven – a considerably more trustworthy safeguard than the police – when these gentlemen confine themselves to destroying each other, as last night, when two rival gangs met and literally massacred each other. The cause of the conflict? As usual, a woman. This one, a prostitute surnamed Desfontaines, known as 'Copper-Nob' on account of her magnificent red hair, inflames all the lustful desires of the shady male characters of the underworld. Inscribed a year ago on the police register, this creature, who numbers barely sixteen springs, is well-known locally for her equivocal charm and her audacious character. She boxes, wrestles and, in case of need, can effectively use a revolver. Brazille, known as The Moth, head of the gang of the Brothers of Belleville, and Curly, head of the Aristos of Levallois-Perret, a dangerous pimp whose real name is unknown, were quarrelling tonight over the favours of Copper-Nob. From threats, they proceeded to knives. Sidney, known as the Viper, a Belgian deserter, grievously wounded, called Curly to his aid; the acolytes of The Moth brought out their revolvers and then commenced a veritable slaughter. The police, arriving after the fight according to their invariable custom, gathered up five persons left for dead: Defrémont and Busenel, Jules Bouquet, known as Bright-Eye, and Blaquy, known as The Mug, were immediately transported to hospital, as also King Leopold's subject, Sidney the Viper.

As to the gang-leaders and the Columbine, the original cause of the duel, no one has been able to lay hands on them. The search for them is being vigorously pursued.

Mamma was rolling up her embroidery. Swiftly, the newspaper vanished under the exercise-book, in which Minne proceeded to scribble a few extra lines at random:

'By this treaty, France lost two of her best provinces. But some time afterwards she was to sign a far more advantageous one.'

Full stop – an ink line ruled at the bottom of her history essay – the blotting-paper smoothed with her transparent hand – and Minne exclaimed triumphantly:

'Finished!'

'And high time too!' said Mamma, with relief. 'Off with you to bed, white mouse! You were very long over it tonight. Was it a very difficult essay?'

'No,' replied Minne, getting up. 'But I've got a bit of a headache.'

How tall she is! Almost as tall as Mamma. An immensely elongated little girl, a child of ten who has been stretched and stretched. Narrow and flat as a board in her tight-fitting high-waisted green velvet dress, Minne made herself longer still by stretching her arms up. She ran her hands over her forehead and pushed back her pale hair. Mamma asked anxiously:

'Does it hurt? Would you like a compress?'

'No,' said Minne. 'It's not worth the bother. It'll be gone tomorrow.'

She smiled at Mamma with her dark brown, almost black eyes and with her mobile mouth, whose sensitive corners were twitching. Her skin was so light and her hair so fine at the roots that you could not see where the temples ended. Mamma examined that little face, every vein of which she knew by heart, from close to and once again worried about its extreme frailty. 'No one would ever think she was four-teen and eight months . . .'

'Come here, Minne darling, so that I can do up your ring-lets.'

She displayed a little bundle of white ribbons.

'Oh, please no, Mamma. Not tonight, because of my headache.'

'You're right, my precious. Would you like me to come up to your room with you? Do you want me for anything?'

'No, thank you, Mamma. I'll get into bed quickly.'

Minne took one of the two oil-lamps, kissed Mamma and went upstairs. She was not afraid of the dark corners nor of the shadow of the banisters which grew larger and swivelled round in front of her, nor of the eighteenth step which creaked lugubriously. At fourteen and eight months one no longer believes in ghosts.

'Five!' thought Minne. 'The police picked up five of them, left for dead. And the Belgian, too, who got badly hurt. But they didn't get *her*, Copper-Nob, nor the two gang leaders, thank goodness!'

In her white nainsook petticoat and her white coutil stay-bodice, Minne studied herself in the looking-glass.

'Copper-Nob! Red hair, that's lovely! Mine is too pale. I know how they do their hair.'

With both hands, she swept up her silky hair and rolled and pinned it into a very high, flaunting puff, almost over her forehead. Going over to a cupboard, she took out the pink apron that she wore in the mornings, the one with the heart-shaped pockets. Then, with her chin in the air, she interrogated the glass. No, the whole effect was still insipid. What more was needed? A red ribbon in the hair. There! Another round the neck, with a bow at the side. And then, with her hands in the apron-pockets, leaving her skinny wrists visible, Minne smiled at her charming, gawky self in the glass and decided, with conviction:

'I'm sinister.'

Minne never went to sleep at once. Down below she heard Mamma shut the piano, pull the curtains which grated on their rings, push the kitchen door ajar to make sure that no smell of gas was escaping from the taps of the cooker, then come slowly upstairs, heavily cluttered by her lamp, her work-basket and her long skirt.

Outside Minne's bedroom, Mamma stopped for a moment, listening ... Finally, the last door closed and nothing more could be heard but muffled sounds behind the wall.

Minne was stretching out quite stiff in her bed with her head thrown back. She could feel her eyes growing bigger in the dark. She was not frighened. She listened to every sound like a little nocturnal animal, rigidly still except for scratching the sheet with her toenails.

On the zinc window-ledge a drop of rain fell from second to second, heavy and regular as the step of the police-sergeant who was pacing the pavement.

'He irritates me, that police-sergeant!' thought Minne. 'What's the use of these people who walk so heavily? The – the Brothers of Belleville and the Aristos – you don't hear *them,* they walk like cats. They have tennis-shoes or else slippers embroidered in *petit-point.* How it rains! I'm sure they're not out at this hour. Yet where are they, The Moth and the other one, the leader of the Brothers – Curly? Escaped, hidden in – in quarries. I don't know if there are any quarries about here. Oh! that heavy step! Plon, plon, plon, plon. And suppose, all at once, one of them were to come up behind him and stick a knife into the back of that sergeant's ugly neck! Outside the front door, just as he was passing! Oh! I can just hear Célénie tomorrow morning: "Madam! Madam! There's been a policeman killed outside the front door!" Ten to one she'd faint!'

And Minne, snuggled down in her white bed, her silky hair swept to one side, revealing one small ear, fell asleep with a little smile.

Minne was asleep and Mamma lay awake thinking. That slender little girl sleeping next door to her fills and limits the entire horizon of Madame . . . What does her name matter? This timid, stay-at-home young widow has only one true appellation: Mamma. Ten years ago, Mamma believed that she had suffered very much when her husband died suddenly; since then that great grief had paled in the gilded shadow of frail, highly-strung Minne's fair hair. Minne's meals, Minne's classes, Minne's clothes left her no time to think of anything else. Mamma was wholly preoccupied with them with a joy and an anxiety both so acute that neither could take the edge off the other.

Nevertheless, Mamma was only thirty-three and men in the street sometimes noticed her discreet beauty, almost extinguished by her schoolmistressy clothes. Mamma was quite unaware of this. She smiled when admiring glances were cast at Minne's amazing hair or blushed violently when some blackguard addressed her daughter. There were no other events in her busy life of a mother-ant. Give Minne a step-father? The idea was unthinkable! No, no, they would go on living all alone in the little house in the Rue Berthier which Papa had left to his wife and daughter . . . all alone until the time, vague and terrifying as a nightmare, when Minne would go off with some man of her choice.

Uncle Paul was there to keep an eye from time to time on the two of them, to look after Minne if she was ill and prevent Mamma from losing her head; Cousin Antoine was there to be company for Minne during the holidays. Minne attended classes at the school run by the Demoiselles Souhait, in order to keep her amused, give her the chance of meeting well-brought-up girls and even – occasionally! – learn something. 'It's all so nicely arranged,' thought Mamma, who dreaded the unforeseen. And if only they could go on like that to the end of their lives, bound close together in a mild restricted happiness, how swiftly and easily death would come, free from sin and free from pain!

'Minne darling, it's half past seven.'

Mamma announced this in a hushed voice, as if apologizing for doing so.

In the white shadow of the bed, a thin arm shot up, clenched its fist, then dropped back again.

Then Minne's faint, light voice enquired:

'Is it still raining?'

Mamma folded back the iron shutters. The rustle of the sycamore trees came in through the window, along with a bright green ray of daylight and a cool breeze that smelt of fresh air and asphalt.

'A glorious day!'

Minne, sitting up in bed, rumpled the tangled silken threads of her hair. Against its lightness and the rosy pallor of her face, the black, liquid lustre of her eyes was startling. Beautiful eyes, wide open and sombre, into which everything sank deep and drowned, under the elegant arch of the melancholy eyebrows. The flexible mouth smiled, but the eyes remained serious. Looking at them, Mamma remembered Minne as a tiny child; a delicate baby who was all white, white skin, white frock, white downy hair – a silver chick who opened a pair of amazing eyes, severe, obstinate and as black as the round disc of water in a well.

At the moment, Minne was staring at the flickering leaves with a blank expression. She kept spreading out her toes and bringing them together again as a cockchafer does its antennae. She had not yet emerged from the night. Her mind was still wandering on in pursuit of her dreams: she did not even hear her loving Mamma walking about the room. Mamma, who was looking delightfully fresh in her blue dressing-gown, with her hair in plaits, said:

'Your yellow boots, and then your little navy-blue skirt and a blouse . . . what kind of blouse?'

Awake at last, Minne sighed and relaxed her stare.

'Blue, Mamma. Or white. Just as you like.'

As if speaking had loosened her limbs, Minne bounded out of bed, went over to the window and leant out: there was no police-sergeant lying across the pavement with a knife in the back of his neck.

'It'll be some other time,' Minne told herself, slightly disappointed.

The vanilla smell of chocolate drifted into the room and made her hurry on with her toilet, the meticulous toilet of an exquisitely groomed little person. She smiled at the pink flowers on the hangings. Roses everywhere: on the walls, on the velvet of the armchairs, on the cream-coloured carpet and even at the bottom of that long basin mounted on four white enamelled legs. Mamma had superstitiously wanted Minne to have roses, roses everywhere about her, to sleep surrounded by roses.

'I'm hungry!' said Minne, as she knotted her tie over a white collar glistening with starch.

What luck! Minne was hungry! Now Mamma would be happy for the entire day. She gazed admiringly at her tall daughter, so tall and still so little of a woman with that childish torso under the pleated blouse and those frail shoulders over which the lovely hair hung in shining ringlets.

'Let's go down, your chocolate's all ready for you.'

Minne took her hat from Mamma's hands and bounded headlong downstairs, nimble as a white goat. As she ran, full of the happy ingratitude which beautifies spoilt children, she sniffed at her handkerchief on which Mamma had poured two drops of lemon verbena.

The classes run by the Demoiselles Souhait are not just a joke. Ask all the mothers who take their daughters to them and they will reply: 'They are the best attended in Paris!' And they will quote, one after another, the names of Mademoiselle X, the little Z girls, the only daughter of H the banker. They will tell you of the well-aired rooms, the steam heating, the lordly cars parked outside the door, and it is almost unheard of for a Mamma, seduced by this hygienic luxury and dazzled by well-known and impressive names, to venture to find fault with the educational programme.

Every morning Minne, accompanied sometimes by Mamma, sometimes by Célénie, followed the fortifications as far as the Boulevard Malesherbes where the Souhait Institute holds its sessions. Neatly gloved, a satchel under her arm, upright and serious, she would bestow a glance on the green, countrified Avenue Gourgaud and a caress on the dogs and children of the painter Thaulow who rambled about freely as lords and masters of the deserted avenue.

Minne knew and envied those free, fair-haired children, those little Scandinavian pirates who spoke a guttural Norwegian among themselves. 'Allowed out all alone, without a nurse, the whole length of the fortifications! But they're too young, all they do is play games. They're not interested in interesting things.'

Arthur Dupin, the stylist of the *Journal*, had confected another masterpiece:

MORE NEWS OF OUR APACHES! IMPORTANT CAPTURE
CURLY ELUDES ALL SEARCH

Still present in the minds of our readers is the gloomy and fully-authenticated story of the night of Tuesday–Wednesday. Since then the police have not remained inactive and twenty-four hours had not elapsed before Inspector Joyeaux laid hands on Vandermeer, known as The Eel. Denounced by one of the wounded transported to hospital, he was run to earth and arrested in furnished lodgings in the Rue de Norvins. Of Copper-Nob, no news. It would seem that even her most intimate friends do not know her whereabouts and we are informed that anarchy reigns among this populace deprived of its queen. Up to now, Curly has succeeded in eluding all search.

Minne, before getting into bed, had just re-read the *Journal* before throwing it into her waste-paper basket. She was a long time getting to sleep, thinking excitedly:

'*She* is hidden, she, their queen! probably also in a quarry.

19

The police don't know how to search. *She* has faithful friends who bring her cold meat and hard-boiled eggs at night. If they discover her hide-out, she'll still have time to kill several policemen before they arrest her. But now her people have mutinied! And the Aristos of Levallois are going to break up too, without Curly to lead them. They ought to have elected a deputy queen to govern in Copper-Nob's absence.'

For Minne all this is as prodigious and as simple as an old-fashioned novel. She knows, beyond a shadow of doubt, that the bare rim of the fortifications is a foreign country swarming with a dangerous and attractive race of savages, a race very different from ours, easily recognizable by the distinctive badges they wear: the cyclist's cap and the black jersey striped with vivid colours, so skin-tight that it looks like a gaudy tattoo. The race produces two distinct types:

1. The Stocky, whose thick hands dangle as he walks and looks like raw steaks and whose hair grows so low on his forehead that it seems to weigh down his eyebrows.

2. The Svelte. This one walks indolently, without making the slightest sound. His Richelieu slippers, which he often replaces by tennis-shoes, display gaudy socks, sometimes holey, sometimes not. Sometimes too, instead of socks, you see the delicate skin of the bare ankle, of a somewhat grubby white, veined with blue. Supple locks of hair curve forward like kiss-curls over the well-shaven cheeks and the pallor of the complexion sets off the feverish red of the lips.

According to Minne's classification, this latter individual embodies the noble type of the mysterious race. The Stocky likes to sing; he walks about with bare-headed girls as gay as himself on his arm. The Svelte thrusts his hands into the pockets of his wide trousers and smokes, his eyes half-closed, while at his side an inferior and furious female screams, weeps and reproaches. 'She is boring him with a mass of little domestic worries,' Minne imagines. '*He* isn't even listening. He is dreaming, he is following the smoke of his oriental cigarette.'

For Minne's reveries do not include the vulgar gasper and for her there are only exotic oriental cigarettes.

Minne marvels how patriarchal this singular race is by day in its habits. When she returns from her class, about noon, she sees any number of 'them' lying stretched out asleep on the grassy slope. The females of the tribe, squatting on their heels, darn clothes and keep silent, or eat a picnic lunch, with greaseproof paper spread over their knees. The strong, handsome males sleep. Some of the ones who are awake have taken off their jackets and are keeping their muscles supple by friendly wrestling bouts.

Minne compares them to cats who, by day, sleep, groom their fur till it shines and sharpen their curved claws on the parquet. The quiescence of cats is like an expectant waiting for something. When night comes, they are howling demons and their screams, like the screams of children being strangled, sometimes reach Minne and disturb her sleep.

The mysterious race does not scream at night: it whistles. Terrible, piercing blasts of whistles sound from near and far in the outer Boulevard, carrying messages from post to post in an incomprehensible system of telephony. When she hears them, Minne shudders from head to heels as if she had been run through by a needle.

'They've whistled twice – a kind of quavering *whee-whee-whee* answered far away, over there. Does that mean: *"Run for your life"*? or: *"The deed is done"*? Perhaps they've done someone in, they've killed an old lady. The old lady is now lying on the floor at the foot of her bed "in a pool of blood". *They* are going to count the gold and the notes, get drunk on red wine and get some sleep. Tomorrow, on the grass bank, they'll tell their comrades about the old lady and share out the booty.

'But, alas! their queen is not there and anarchy reigns; the *Journal* said so! Oh, to be their Queen, with a red ribbon and a revolver, to understand the whistle language, to stroke Curly's hair and tell them what crimes to commit. Queen Minne! Queen Minne! Why not? After all, they say Queen Wilhelmina.'

Minne, already asleep, was still rambling on . . .

Today being Sunday, Uncle Paul came to lunch as he did every Sunday, bringing his son Antoine with him.

Mamma had arranged this little family feast as daintily as a dolls' dinner-party. There was a bunch of roses in the middle of the table and a strawberry tart on the sideboard. This smell of strawberries and roses led the conversation towards the coming summer holidays; Mamma was thinking of the orchard where Minne would play in the good sunshine; her brother Paul was hoping that the change of air would benefit his liver. He smiled at Mamma whom he always treated as a little sister: his long, hollow face seemed to be carved out of knotty box-wood. Mamma spoke to him deferentially, inclining her neck, tightly sheathed in the high white collar, in agreement with everything he said. She was wearing a depressing grey voile frock which made her look more than ever like a young woman dressed as a grandmother. She had preserved a childish respect for this hypochondriac brother who had lived for many years on the other side of the world, treated Negroes and Chinese and had brought back from those parts a congested liver which turned his face a bilious green, as well as various types of fever.

Antoine would have liked to take another helping of ham and salad but he dared not. He dreaded his father's disapproving little whistle and the inevitable comment: 'My boy, if you think you'll get rid of your pimples by stuffing yourself with salted meat . . .' Antoine abstained and surreptitiously observed Minne. Though he was three years older, he became acutely self-conscious the moment Minne's black eyes rested on him: he felt his pimples reddening and his ears turning scarlet and hastily swallowed large glasses of water.

Seventeen is a very difficult age for a boy and Antoine was painfully enduring his awkward adolescence. The black school uniform with its little gilt buttons weighed on him like a humiliating livery and the down which darkened his cheeks and upper lip made people wonder: 'Does he already need to shave or hasn't he washed yet?' Schoolboys require endless patience to endure so much uncomeliness. This particular one, tall, with an equine nose and well-set grey eyes would no doubt make a handsome man, but the handsome man was hatching out in the skin of a rather ugly hobble-dehoy.

Antoine despatched his salad in cautious mouthfuls, thinking: 'My aunt has a mania for serving Cos lettuce cut lengthways: it's a beastly nuisance to eat! If I get a leaf stuck between my lips, Minne will say I eat like a goat. It's incredible what cheek girls have, putting on that act of saying nothing! What's the matter with her again this morning? Staring into the distance with her eyes popping out of her head! She hasn't uttered a word since the boiled eggs. What manners!'

He laid his knife and fork down on his plate, wiped his black-shadowed mouth and gave Minne a cold, arrogant stare. While she appeared to disdain it – and with what haughtiness! – he thought:

'I don't care. She's prettier than Bouquetet's sister. They can make as much fun of her as they like at school because, in photos, her hair comes out white; they've none of them got cousins who look so smashing and so frightfully distinguished. That clot Bouquetet thinks she's too thin! Perhaps she is, but I'm not like him. I don't judge women by their weight.'

Minne was sitting facing broad daylight. The reflections of the leaves and of the Boulevard Berthier, white as a country road, made her look paler still. Absent-minded and preoccupied all morning, she stared unblinkingly at the dazzling window with the tranced concentration of a sleep-walker. She was following her familiar visions, nightmares imagined at length, pictures re-composed a hundred times, varying in minute details: the reviled and feared Tribe, the combined force of the Sveltes and the Stockies, is assaulting a terrified Paris. One night, about eleven, the windows are smashed, hands armed with knives and coshes overturn the peaceful table and the guardian lamp. They slaughter at random, to the sound of quiet death-rattles and the soft thuds of their cat-like springs. Then, in the darkness reddened by the flames of the burning house, the hands snatch Minne up, carrying her away with irresistible force, one knows not whither.

'Minne, darling, a little tart?'

'Yes, please, Mamma.'

'And some caster sugar?'

'No, thank you, Mamma.'

Worried by her Minne looking pale and absent-minded, Mamma drew Uncle Paul's attention to her daughter by jerking her chin in her direction. Uncle Paul shrugged his shoulders.

'Pooh! The child's perfectly well. A little run down from growing so fast . . . it takes it out of them.'

'It's not dangerous?'

'No, of course not. She's a girl who's developing late, that's all. What does that matter to you? You don't want to get her married this year, do you?'

'Me? Good heavens, what an idea!'

Mamma covered her ears with both hands and shut her eyes as if she had seen a flash of lightning strike the opposite side of the Boulevard Berthier.

'What are you laughing at, Minne?' asked Uncle Paul.

'Me?'

Minne at last unfixed her gaze from the open window.

'I wasn't laughing, Uncle Paul.'

'Oh yes you were, you little monkey.'

His long bony hand gave a friendly tug to one of Minne's sausage-curls, pulling it out into silvery-gold spirals and letting it spring back into a smooth shining ringlet.

'You're still laughing! It's this idea of your getting married, eh?'

'No,' said Minne truthfully. 'I was laughing at another idea . . .'

'My idea,' continued Minne in the depths of herself, 'is that the papers don't know anything or that they're paid to keep quiet. I've searched through all the pages of the *Journal* without Mamma seeing me. All the same it's jolly convenient having a mother like mine who never sees anything!'

Yes, it is certainly convenient. It is very obvious that the insoluble problem of a young girl's education has never vexed Mamma's artless soul. For nearly fifteen years Mamma has never trembled before Minne except with fear and admiration. What mysterious design had formed this female child in her – this alarmingly well-behaved child who spoke little and seldom laughed, who was secretly in love with drama, with romantic adventure, with passion – the passion of which she knew nothing and which was only a word to her, a hissing word that she whispered under her breath as if testing the new lash of a whip? Nevertheless, this cold child who knew neither fear nor pity and gave herself in imagination to bloodthirsty heroes, carefully avoided upsetting the naïve susceptibilities of that tender guardian, that nun dedicated only to the worship of Minne, her mother. She handled her with the most delicate diplomacy, slightly tinged with contempt.

It was not out of fear that Minne hid her thoughts from her mother. A charitable instinct warned her to remain in Mamma's eyes a good little girl who was getting a big girl now, as fastidiously clean as a white cat, who said 'Yes, Mamma,' and 'No, Mamma,' who attended classes and went to bed at half past nine. 'I'd frighten her,' said Minne to herself, gazing at her mother, who was pouring the coffee into the cups, with her calm, unfathomable eyes.

July suddenly turned hot. The Tribe panted in the meagre shade under Minne's windows and on the bald slope of the grass bank. The few benches in the Boulevard Berthier were cumbered with sleeping men, lying dead still, with their caps pulled down over their eyes like a mask, hiding the tops of their faces. Minne, in a white linen frock, with a big shady straw hat pulled down over her light hair, would pass quite close to them, close enough to brush against their sleeping forms. She tried to make out the masked faces and told herself, 'They're asleep. You don't read about anything in the papers these days, except suicides and sunstrokes. It's the dead season.'

Mamma, who was taking Minne to her class, kept making her change over to the opposite pavement and sighing:

'This neighbourhood isn't fit to live in!'

Minne did not open her eyes wide and ask innocently: 'Why not, Mamma?' Such little tricks were unworthy of her.

Now and then, they met a lady, a friend of Mamma's, and stopped to chat for five minutes. Naturally they talked about Minne, who smiled politely and held out a hand with long, slender fingers. And Mamma would say:

'Yes, she really has grown some more since Easter. Oh! she's a great big baby! If you knew what a child she is still! I wonder how such a little girl will ever manage to grow up!'

And the lady, much touched, would venture to stroke the lovely hair with its pearly sheen, tied up with a white ribbon. Meanwhile, the 'great big baby' who had raised her beautiful black eyes and was smiling again was ferociously commenting inwardly:

'That lady's stupid! She's ugly. She has a little mole on her cheek and she calls it a beauty-spot. She must smell horrid when she's naked. Yes, that's it. I'd like her to be quite naked in the street and get carried off by Them. And then they're to draw fatal signs with the point of a knife on her ugly bottom! And then they must drag her off, as yellow as rancid butter, and dance the war-dance on her body and throw her into a lime-kiln!'

Minne, ready dressed to go out, was fidgeting in her white bedroom, so nervous that she was on the point of stamping. Célénie, the fat housemaid, was keeping her waiting. Suppose *he* were gone!

For four days now, Minne had been meeting *him* at the corner of the Avenue Gourgaud and the Boulevard Berthier. The first day, he was asleep sitting down, leaning back against the wall and blocking half the pavement. Célénie, frightened, tugged at Minne's sleeve; but Minne – she is so absent-minded! – had already brushed against the feet of the sleeper, who opened his eyes. Such eyes! They gave Minne the shock and thrill of absolute, unqualified admiration. Black, almond-shaped eyes whose whites looked bluish in a face of Italian pallor. A delicate moustache, as if drawn in ink, and black hair all curly with moisture. In order to sleep, he had thrown off his black and purple check cap and his right hand had a dead cigarette clipped between the thumb and the first finger.

He stared at Minne, without budging, with such outrageously flattering effrontery that she very nearly stopped dead.

That day Minne got *five* for history, and as they say at the Souhait establishment: 'Five is a disgrace!' Minne heard herself being publicly reprimanded while, looking very meek and with her eyes elsewhere, she silently assigned Mademoiselle Souhait to complicated and ignominious tortures.

Every day at noon, Minne brushed against the loafer and the loafer stared at Minne, in her white summer frock, who gazed straight back at him with her serious eyes. She thought: 'He's waiting for me. He loves me. He's understood me. How can I let him know that I'm never free? If only I could slip him a note, I'd write: *I am a prisoner. Kill Célénie and we'll go away together.* Go away together ... into his life ... into a life where I wouldn't even remember that I'm Minne ...'

She was slightly astonished at the inertia of her elegant,

shirtless and sockless 'ravisher' who seemed to do nothing but doze at the foot of a sycamore. But, on thinking it over, she found a satisfactory explanation of his apparent list-lessness and his pallor which was like that of grass grown under a stone: 'How many did he kill last night?' She gave a furtive glance to see if she could find any traces of blood on the finger-nails of the unknown ... No blood! Slender fingers, too pointed, and always a cigarette, alight or extinct, between the thumb and first finger. A beautiful cat, whose eyes keep watch under the sleeping eyelids! How terrible his spring would be as he pounced to slay Célénie and carry off Minne!

Mamma, too, had noticed the unknown man at midday. She quickened her step and blushed and heaved a long sigh when the peril was passed and the Avenue Gourgaud safely crossed.

'Do you often see that man sitting on the ground, Minne?'

'A man sitting on the ground?'

'Don't turn round! A man sitting on the ground at the corner of the Avenue. I'm always afraid that those sort of people are lying in wait to commit some crime in the neigh-bourhood!'

Minne made no reply. All her small secret self swelled with pride. 'It's me he's lying in wait for! It's only for me that he's there! Mamma can't understand.'

About the eighth day, Minne was struck by an idea which she promptly recognized as a revelation: that mat pallor, that black, curly hair ... it was Curly! It was Curly himself! The papers had said so: 'They have not succeeded in cap-turing Curly ...' He is at the corner of the Boulevard Berthier and the Avenue Gourgaud, Curly is in love with Minne and every day he risks his life for her.

Minne palpitated with excitement. She could no longer sleep and got up in the night to look for Curly's shadow under her window.

'This can't go on for long,' she told herself. 'One night he'll whistle under the window. I shall descend by a ladder or a knotted rope and he will carry me off on a motor-cycle to the quarries where his assembled subjects will be awaiting him. He will say: "Here is your Queen!" And ... and ... it will be terrible!'

One day, Curly was missing at the rendezvous. Mamma was heartbroken that Minne ate no lunch. But the next day and the next and all the following days there was no somnolent, supple Curly who opened his eyes so suddenly when Minne brushed against him.

Oh! Minne's presentiments! '*I* knew very well that he was Curly! And now he's in prison, perhaps on the way to the guillotine!' Faced with Minne's inexplicable tears and a rise in her temperature, Mamma, nearly out of her wits, sent for Uncle Paul, who prescribed soup, chicken, a light tonic wine and immediate departure to the country.

While Mamma was packing the trunks with the feverish activity of an ant that feels a storm coming, Minne, idle and sorrowful, pressed her forehead against the window-pane and dreamed. 'He is in prison for my sake. He is suffering for my sake. He is languishing in his cell and writing love-poems: *To an unknown girl.*'

Minne, woken up with a start by the grinding of a pulley, opened her eyes and stared with alarm at the peaceful bedroom: 'Where am I?'

Though she had arrived three days ago at Uncle Paul's, Minne had still not got used to his house in the country. Emerging from her restless sleep, peopled with hazy dreams, she still instinctively expected to see the clear blue dusk of her Paris bedroom and smell the lemony scent of her toilet-water. Here, because of the solid shutters, it was black night, in spite of the crowing cocks and the clatter of crockery coming up from the dining-room where Célénie was laying the table for breakfast. Thick darkness, pierced only by one pencil-thin streak of bright gold over by the window.

Guided by this little glittering streak, Minne groped her way, barefooted, over to the window and opened the shutters. She drew back, blinded by the light, and stood there, with her hands over her eyes. In her long nightdress, she looked like a repentant angel.

When the sunlight had pierced the pink shell of her hand, she went back to her bed, sat down on it and, clasping one bare foot, smiled at the window where the wasps were dancing. Now, with her mouth half open and her eyes all innocence, she resembled a baby on the cover of an English magazine. But the eyebrows lowered, and a sudden thought came into the wide eyes which misted over like a lake. Minne was thinking that not everyone was enjoying this buzzing sunlight, that somewhere in a great city was a dark cell where an unknown man with black curly hair lay on his pallet, dreaming.

All the same, one had to dress, go downstairs, sip the

frothing milk, laugh, enquire after Uncle Paul's health. 'That's life!' sighed Minne, combing her hair which the sun filtered through and lit up as if it were spun glass.

The floor groaned under Minne's light step. If she stayed still, the Empire armchairs stretched their limbs, cracked their joints and made sudden explosive noises. The wooden bed replied. The dried-up, resonant house crackled as if it were invisibly on fire. It had stood for two hundred years in the sun and the wind and its warm timber was perpetually creaking and groaning. It was known in the neighbourhood as the Dry House.

Minne loved it for its vast size, for its drawing-room, separated from the garden only by a flight of five stone steps, for its white wooden floors that were warm to bare feet, for the twenty-seven acres of park and orchard that surrounded it. As a little Parisian accustomed to unobtrusive colours, she was amazed that all these crude clashing ones in her bedroom so delighted her eyes. The wall-paper had deep pink stripes, the chintz counterpane was trellised with blue convolvuluses and green garlands, orange muslin curtains hung at the windows and the bignonia, heavy with flowers, swayed flaming clusters right into the room. Minne, pale as a moonlight night, warmed herself at this blaze of colours, which she could almost feel scorching her skin. Now and then, standing quite naked in the sunlight with a mirror in her hand, she tried in vain to see right through her slim body and make out the darker shadow of her elegant skeleton.

'A letter for you, Minne . . . That's *Femina*, that's the *Journal de la Santé*, then there's the *Chronique Médicale*, and then a circular.'

'Isn't there anything for me?' implored Antoine.

Uncle Paul's yellow face emerged from the bowl of milk he was holding in both hands:

'My poor boy, you really are extraordinary! You don't write to anyone so why do you expect anyone to write to you? Have the goodness to answer me.'

'I don't know,' said Antoine.

His father's witticism irritated him: Minne's superior irony exasperated him. She was taking no part in the discussion, she was drinking her milk in little sips, taking a new breath from time to time and staring fixedly at the open window as she used to do in the Boulevard Berthier. The green of the garden was strangely reflected in her black eyes.

'All that proud, just because she's got a letter!' thought Antoine.

Proud? It hardly seemed so. She put the closed envelope down by her plate and finished her bowl of milk before opening it.

'Come and look, Minne,' called Antoine who was leafing through *Femina*. 'It's smashing. There are photos of the Journée des Drags . . . Oh! you can see Polaire!'

'Who's Polaire?' Minne deigned to ask.

Antoine roared with laughter, suddenly getting the upper hand again:

'You really mean to say you don't know Polaire?'

Minne's dreamy little face became suspicious:

'No. Do you?'

'When I say *know*, of course I don't mean I know her to speak to. She's an actress. I saw her at a charity performance. She was with three others; she played a street-walker.'

'Antoine!' Madame scolded gently.

'Sorry, Aunt. I mean a woman of the outer Boulevards.'

Minne's eyes widened and lit up.

'Ah! How was she dressed?'

'She looked smashing! A red bodice, an apron and then, her hair like that, right down over her eyes, and then a cap ...'

'What do you mean, a cap?' interrupted Minne, shocked at the inexactness of detail.

'Yes, a silk one, very high. That was just what it was.'

Minne turned away, no longer interested.

'*I* shouldn't have worn a cap,' she said simply.

She looked at Antoine mechanically, without seeing him. He fidgeted, embarrassed by Minne's beauty and the diabolical little flame in her dark eyes. He thrust a badly-folded handkerchief into his pocket where it made a bulge, brushed the down on his lip with the back of his hand and picked up the straw hat with the shady brim that he had flung under the chair.

'I'm going to eat some plums,' he announced.

'Not too many!' implored Mamma.

'Don't fuss,' said Uncle Paul behind his newspaper. 'They'll open his bowels.'

Antoine blushed violently and fled from the room as if his father had cursed him.

Minne got up from the table and tied the strings of a linen sun-bonnet under her chin. She was wearing her pink apron and the sun-bonnet made her look younger still. All demure sweetness, she held out the blue letter to Mamma:

'Keep my letter for me, Mamma. It's from Henriette Deslandres, the girl who sits next to me in class. You can read it, you know, Mamma. I haven't got any secrets. Good-bye, Mamma. I'm going to eat some plums.'

The grass in the orchard was dazzling, all its varnished,

sharp-edged blades glittered. Minne traversed it in great strides as if she were plunging her way through running water, sending up splashes of hundreds of grasshoppers, blue in the air, grey on the ground. The sun beat down through Minne's sun-bonnet, scorching her shoulders with such fierce heat that she shivered. Wild parsnips spread out their white umbrellas and incensed Minne as she passed with their sickly-sweet smell. Minne was hurrying because the points of the grass-blades that pierced through her stockings pricked her: suppose they were stinging insects?

The undulating meadow was pitted with hollow dells where the grass looked blue; above the half-ruined stone fence the little round, symmetrical mountains seemed to continue the rolling swell of the land.

'Isn't that Antoine an idiot not to have waited for me? Suppose a snake came along while I was all alone? Oh well, I'd try to tame it. You whistle, and they come. But how would I know if it was a viper or a grass-snake?'

Antoine was sitting on the flat rocks which showed just above the soil, almost flush with it. He had seen Minne coming, pressed two fingers against his temple and assumed a noble, pensive expression.

'Ah, 'tis thee!' he exclaimed theatrically.

'It's me. Whatever are you doing?'

'Nothing. I was thinking.'

'I don't want to disturb you.'

Terrified at seeing her about to go away, he answered awkwardly that 'there's room for two in the orchard!'

Minne sat down on the ground and untied her sun-bonnet to let the wind get at her ears. She considered Antoine carefully and dispassionately, with no more regard for his feelings than if he were a piece of furniture.

'You know, Antoine, I like you better like that, in a flannel shirt, without a waistcoat.'

Once again he blushed.

'Oh, you think so? I look better than in uniform?'

'You certainly do. Only that straw hat makes you look like a gardener.'

34

'Thanks!'

'What I'd like better,' Minne went on, without even hearing him, 'is . . . yes, I know . . . a cap.'

'A cap! Minne, you're cracked!'

'A cyclist's cap, that's it. And then your hair . . . wait!'

She unfolded her legs like a grasshopper, came and fell on her knees close beside him and took off his hat. Troubled by her nearness, he tucked his feet under him and became rude:

'For goodness sake, leave me alone, you beastly kid!'

She smiled with her lips while her serious eyes reflected, right in their depths, the little mountains, the sky white with heat and a swaying branch of the plum-tree. She was combing Antoine's hair with a little pocket-comb, manipulating her cousin with neither pleasure nor girlish modesty, as if he were a puppet.

'Oh, *do* keep still! There! The hair right down like that on the forehead and then brought well forward at the sides. But it's too short at the sides. Never mind, it looks better already. With a black and purple check cap.'

These last words brought back all too vividly the listless sleeper of the fortifications: she fell silent, let go of her puppet and sat down again without saying a word. 'Another of her whims!' thought Antoine.

He said nothing either: he was stirred with resentment and vague longing. This Minne so close to him – he could have counted her eyelashes! – those thin little hands, cold as mice, running their pointed fingers over his temples, in his ears . . . Antoine's big nose quivered in the effort to gather in the last traces of the scent of lemon verbena that hovered in the air. Sitting there, humble and vexed, he awaited some renewal of hostilities. But she was dreaming, her hands folded, gazing vaguely straight ahead, oblivious of Antoine's annoyance, of his Don Quixote-like ugliness: the big, bony, kindly nose, the big eyes, circled with the dark rings of adolescence, the wide, generous mouth with its square, strong teeth, the uneven complexion, with a few inflamed spots on the chin.

Suddenly, Minne woke up, pursed her lips and stuck out a pointed finger.

'Over there!' she said.

'What?'

'Do you see him?'

Antoine pulled the brim of his hat down over his eyes like a visor and said, with a yawn of boredom.

'Yes, I do. It's old Corne. What's come over you?'

'Yes, it's him,' Minne said in a portentous whisper.

She reared herself upright on her slender feet and flung her arms forward, in the attitude of a menacing Fury.

'I hate him!'

Antoine felt another 'whim' coming on. He assumed a neutral expression in which suspicion struggled with pity.

'What's he done to you?'

'What's he done to me? I hate him because he's ugly, because Uncle Paul has lent him a piece of the orchard to plant his vegetables in, because I can't come here any more without running into old Corne who looks like a toad and who has yellow stuff running out of his eyes and who smells nasty and who plants leeks and who ... who ... Lord! how I suffer!'

She writhed her arms like a little girl playing Phèdre. Antoine feared the worst of this maenad. But her expression changed. She sat down again on the flat rock and pulled her frock over her shoes. Her eyes portended gossip and mystery.

'And then, you know, Antoine ...'

'Know what?'

'He's a bad man, old Corne.'

'Dear me, now! Fancy that!'

'There's no question of "Fancy that!"' said Minne crossly. 'You'd do better to believe me and to pull up your socks. Everyone doesn't have to know that you wear long mauve underpants.'

This type of observation invariably plunges Antoine into a prudish irritability which Minne delights in.

'And besides, he plays the flageolet in bed on Sunday mornings!'

Antoine rolled on his back in the grass, like a donkey.

'The flageolet! No, Minne, you really are a scream! He doesn't know how to!'

'I didn't say he knew how to play it. I tell you he plays it. Célénie's seen him. He lies in bed, in a brown woolly, with his loathsome face and his runny eyes, his sheets are dirty and he plays the flageolet . . . Ugh!'

A shudder of horror shook Minne from head to foot.

'Girls are always a bit loopy,' Antoine, who had known old Corne for fifteen years, muttered to himself philosophically. He was a grumpy, slovenly old clerk with sore eyes, the very sight of whom drove Minne into a kind of frenzy of repulsion.

'What could we do to him, Antoine?'

'Do to who?'

'Old Corne.'

'*I* don't know.'

'You never *do* know! Have you got a knife?'

He instinctively put his hand over his trouser-pocket.

'You *have*!' affirmed Minne peremptorily. 'Lend it to me!'

He jeered at her, awkward as a bear confronted with a she-cat.

'Hurry up, Antoine!'

She flung herself on him, plunged a bold hand into the forbidden pocket and took possession of a knife with a boxwood handle. Antoine, his ears crimson, said not a word.

'You see, you liar! It's pretty, your knife! It's like you. Come on, old Corne's gone. We're going to have a game, Antoine! We're going to have a game in old Corne's vegetable garden. The leeks are the enemies, the pumpkins are the fortresses: it's old Corne's army!'

She was brandishing the open knife like a redoubtable little fairy and rambling aloud as she trampled down the lettuces:

'Oooh! Help! Mercy! We'll drag away their corpses and we'll violate them!'

'What?'

'I said we'll violate them. Lord, I'm hot!'

She flung herself flat down on her stomach on a bed of parsley. Antoine stared in stupefaction at this fair-haired child who had just uttered something scandalous.

'I heard you the first time. Do you know what that means?'

'You bet I do.'

'I bet you don't.'

He took off his hat, put it on again and scraped his heel on the drought-cracked earth.

'How maddening you are, Antoine! You're always trying to catch me out. It was Mamma who explained to me what it meant.'

'It was . . . my aunt who . . .'

'One day I read in a lesson: "And their tombs were violated". So I asked Mamma: "What is violating a tomb?" Mamma said: "It's opening it without permission." Well, violating a corpse is opening it without permission. Are you cross? Hark, that's the lunch bell. Are you coming?'

At table, Antoine mopped his brow with his napkin and drank large glasses of water.

'Are you very hot, poor boy?' Mamma asked.

'Yes, Aunt. We did a lot of running about, so . . .'

'Whatever are you saying?' cried that she-devil of a Minne from the end of the table. 'We didn't run about at all. We watched old Corne gardening.'

Uncle Paul shrugged his shoulders.

'Overheated blood. The chap's purple in the face. My boy, you'll do me the favour of starting drinking gentian again: that'll get rid of your pimples for you.'

'That melon isn't going down well,' sighed Uncle Paul, slumped in a cane armchair.

'You've got a weak stomach,' decreed old Luzeau. '*I* take some Combier water before and after my meals and I can eat as much melon and runner-beans as I like.'

Old Luzeau, stiff and upright in a khaki drill shooting

outfit, was smoking his pipe, his eyes peering out from an ambush of reddish hairs. Uncle Paul had a soft spot for this robust wreck and resigned himself once a week to entertaining the pompous, stupid old sportsman to a meal. Old Luzeau belched noisily, smelt of pubs and hare's blood and Minne did not like him.

'He looks a crafty old wretch,' she thought. 'People think he's a decent man, but they don't know what he gets up to in secret. Those eyes! He must carry off little children and feed them to the pigs.'

A still evening lay heavy over the countryside. After dinner, to get away from the lamps encircled by mosquitoes, brown moths with Mephistophelean antennae and little downy hawk-moths with birdlike eyes, Uncle Paul and his guest, Minnie and Antoine had come out to sit on the terrace.

The kitchen fire and the dining-room lamp darted out two pencils of orange light into the garden. The cicadas chirped as loudly as if it were broad daylight and the house which had drunk in the sunshine through all the pores of its grey stone would stay warm till midnight.

Minne and Antoine, sitting, with their legs dangling, on the low wall of the terrace, said not a word. Antoine was trying to make out Minne's eyes in the darkness; but the darkness was so dense. He was hot, he felt uncomfortable in his skin and patiently endured this all-too-familiar sensation.

Minne, motionless, stared straight in front of her. She was listening to the footsteps of night rustling the sand of the garden, and creating appalling faces in the darkness which made her thrill with pleasure. This tranquil, oppressive hour filled her with impatience and, confronted with so much calm beauty, she conjured up the beloved Tribe that ruled her dreams.

This hot, oppressive night, in which one's hands sought the chill of stone! All along the fortifications it would be full of fever and murder, pierced with shrill whistles. Minne turned abruptly towards her cousin.

'Whistle, Antoine!'

'Whistle what?'

'Whistle a great blast, as loud as you can. Louder! Louder! Oh! that's enough! You haven't any idea how to do it!'

Minne clasped her hands, made all the middle joints of her fingers crack and yawned at the moon like a cat.

'What time is it? Isn't that old Luzeau ever going to go?'

'Why? It isn't late. Are you sleepy?'

She made a contemptuous face: sleep!

'That old man gets on my nerves!'

'Everything gets on your nerves! He's a decent chap, but a bit of a bore.'

She shrugged her shoulders and spoke straight ahead of her into the darkness.

'Everyone's a decent chap, according to you. Haven't you ever looked at his eyes? Believe me, I know what I know!'

'Rot. You don't know a thing.'

'You might at least be polite. Who d'you think you're talking to? Old Luzeau is a veteran in crime.'

'A veteran in crime! What, *him*? Minne, suppose he heard you!'

'If he heard me, he'd never dare come back here again! He lures little girls into his little shooting-lodge and then he rapes them and strangles them! That's how the little Quenet girl disappeared.'

'Oh, come now!'

'*Yes.*'

Antoine felt his brain reeling. He burst out, keeping his voice discreetly low:

'But it's not true! You know perfectly well that her parents said that she's run away to Paris with a . . .'

'With a commercial traveller. I know. Old Luzeau paid them not to tell the truth. People like that'll do anything for money.'

Antoine was crushed for a moment, then his common sense revolted. He was sufficiently emboldened to grab Minne's wrists in his rough hands.

'Look here, Minne, one doesn't make such horrible accusations without being sure of the facts! Who told you all this?'

The silvery halo round Minne's invisible face shook in the gusts of her laughter.

'Ha! Ha! D'you think I'd be silly enough to tell you who?'

She freed her wrists and resumed her Infanta-like haughtiness.

'I know plenty of other things, Sir! But I don't trust you enough!'

The big, awkward, tender-hearted boy suddenly felt as if he wanted to cry. He said in a tone of lofty contempt:

'Not trust me! I like that! Have I ever told on you about anything? Only this very morning, when old Corne came and complained about his ruined vegetables, did I blab?'

'It would have been the limit if you had! That's only the first stage.'

'Well then?' implored Antoine.

'Well what?'

'You'll tell me some more?'

He had given up all show of contempt. He bent his tall figure down towards this indifferent little queen who harboured so many secrets under her gold-dust hair.

'I'll see,' she said.

'Can I come in, Antoine?' cried Minne's shrill voice behind the door.

Antoine, scared as a startled virgin, darted from side to side of his bedroom, shouting: 'No! No!' and frantically searching for his tie. There was an impatient scratching and Minnie opened the door.

'What do you mean, "no, no"? Because you're in your shirt-sleeves? My poor boy, if you think *that* embarrasses me!'

Minne, in flax-blue, her hair smooth under the white ribbon, halted in front of her cousin who was nervously knotting the tie he had at last managed to find. She stared at him with her deep, dark eyes in which the reflections of her fine lashes quivered like the reflections of grass in a pool. Gazing at those eyes, Antoine marvelled for a moment, then averted his own. They had the stern candour one sees in the eyes of very young babies, the ones who are so serious because they cannot yet speak. Their dark water engulfed images and because he had seen himself reflected in it for a moment, Antoine, as ill-at-ease in his shirt-sleeves as a warrior without his breast-plate, lost all his self-assurance.

'Why do you put water on your hair?' inquired Minne aggressively.

'To make my parting stay put, of course.'

'It's ugly. You look like a Red Indian with your hair plastered down like that.'

'Oh, so you burst in on me before I'd finished dressing just to tell me that!'

Minne shrugged her shoulders. She wandered round the room, with the air of a lady paying a social call, and, leaning over a glass case, pointed to its contents.

'What's that butterfly?'

He bent down, so close to Minne that her fine hair tickled him.

'It's a Red Admiral.'

'Ah!'

Feeling suddenly immensely brave, Antoine put his arm round Minne's waist. He had no idea what he was going to do next. A lemony scent, light as Minne's hair made his mouth water acidly.

'Minne, why don't you kiss me any more when you say good morning?'

Waking up, she disengaged herself and resumed her pure, grave expression.

'Because it isn't proper.'

'But when there's nobody there – like now?'

Minne stood there, with her hands dangling by her sides, looking thoughtful.

'No, there's nobody here. But I shouldn't enjoy it.'

'How do you know?'

Having spoken, he was alarmed by his audacity. Minne

42

made no reply. The blood rushed into his cheeks as he remembered an afternoon of reading dirty books that had left him throbbing all over, with his ears burning and his hands icy, just as he was at this moment. Minne seemed to make up her mind all of a sudden.

'All right! Kiss me. But I must shut my eyes.'

'Do you think me so ugly?'

Not in the least touched by the sincere, humble cry, she shook her head and her shining ringlets.

'No. But it's take it or leave it.'

She shut her eyes and remained standing rigidly upright, waiting. Now that her black eyes had disappeared she looked suddenly younger and fairer: a little girl asleep. With an ill-calculated dab, Antoine's greedy mouth landed on her cheek. He was about to try again but he felt himself pushed away by two clawed little hands. And the dark eyes, suddenly unveiled, cried wordlessly:

'Get away! You couldn't deceive me. You're not *him*!'

Minne slept badly that night, with the restless sleep of a bird. When she went to bed, a low cloud was advancing from the west like a black wall, the dry, sandy air dessicated the nostrils. Uncle Paul, very ill-at-ease and liverish, had vainly sought an hour's repose on the terrace and then gone upstairs early, leaving Mamma to fasten the shutters and chide Célénie: 'The little door downstairs? – It's always kept locked. – The dormer-window in the attic? – It's never opened. – That's no excuse. I'll go and see for myself.'

Nevertheless Minne had fallen asleep, lulled by dull, muffled rumbling. A sudden crash awakened her, followed by an extraordinary gust of wind which began as a whispering breeze and swelled to a gale that battered the house, making it creak and groan from top to bottom. Then came a great dead calm. But Minne knew that it was not over: she waited, blinded by the blades of blue fire that split the shutters.

She was not afraid, but this physical and mental waiting overstrained her. Her hands and feet were anxious and the tip of her delicate nose quivered with a separate anxiety of its own. She flung off the sheet and pushed her hair back from her forehead, for its tickling, like the strands of a spider's web, got on her nerves till she could have screamed.

Another wave of wind! It rushed on like a Fury and tore round the house, rattling the shutters as insistently as a human hand; Minne could hear the trees groaning. A hollow uproar muffled their moans; the thunder sounded empty and false, flung back in echoes from the little mountains. 'It's not the same thunder as in Paris,' thought Minne, curled up on her uncovered bed. 'I can hear Mamma's bedroom door ... I'd like to see Antoine's face! ... He pretends to be brave in front of other people but he's frightened of thunderstorms. I'd also like to see the trees bending their backs.'

She ran to the window, guided by the lightning flashes. The moment she pushed back the shutters, a blinding blaze struck her and sent her reeling backwards and Minne thought she was dying.

The conviction that she was still alive returned with the darkness. An irresistible wind blew her hair straight up on end and sent the curtains billowing up to the ceiling. Revived, Minne could make out the tortured garden in the fantastic light that blazed out from second to second; the roses, purple in the mauve glare of the lightning, fighting for life, the plane-trees, imploring mercy of an invisible and innumerable host of enemies with their outspread, terrified leafy hands.

'Everything's changed!' thought Minne. She could no longer recognize the peaceful horizon of the mountains in this jagged silhouette of Japanese peaks, now greenish, now pink, from which a glittering tree of lightning shot up one after another, making it momentarily part of the tragic sky.

Minne, in an ecstasy, flung herself into the storm, into the theatrical light and the majestic rumbling with her whole soul, that soul in love with violence and mystery. She would have gathered fearlessly those death-dealing tree-ferns and leapt on to the fire-edged clouds, providing that she could have been rewarded with one insulting, flattering glance from under Curly's languid lids. She had a confused apprehension of the joy of dying for someone, in front of someone, and that it would be easy to be brave provided you had a little pride to help you or a little love . . .

Antoine, his face in his pillow, clenched his jaws hard enough to crack the enamel of his teeth. The approach of the storm sent him crazy. He was all alone, he could writhe as much as he wanted to and stifle in the warm feathers rather than look at the lightning flashes and hope with the fervour of an explorer dying of thirst for the first drops of the appeasing shower.

He was not afraid, no, – not positively. But it was too much for him. Nevertheless, the extreme violence of the storm succeeded in distracting his selfish apprehension from himself. Sitting bolt upright, he listened. 'I'm sure that one just now fell in the orchard! Minne must be dying of fright!'

Conjuring up a clear-cut picture of a panic-stricken Minne, pale in her white nightdress, her hair a shower of silver mingled with gold, sent a stream of amorous and heroic thoughts coursing through Antoine's mind. Oh, to save Minne! To rush to her room, clasp her in his arms at the very moment when she had no voice left to call for help. To crush her against him and revive that cold little body, whose thinness had hardly begun to develop any feminine curves, under his caresses! Antoine, with his legs out of bed, and his head bowed to protect his face from the lightning flashes that struck it like blows, no longer knew whether he was escaping from the storm or rushing to Minne till, all at once, the sight of his long legs, hard and hairy as a faun's, checked his impulse: could anyone imagine a hero in a night-shirt?

While he was hesitating, by turns excited and shy, the storm moved away and died down to a distant rumble of artillery. One by one the first drops of the deluge fell, bouncing off the leaves of the clematis as if off taut drums. An exquisite languor overwhelmed Antoine and loosened all his limbs with the beneficial oil of laziness.

Minne no longer appeared under the aspect of a pathetic victim but under the aspect – no less disturbing – of a young girl in her nightdress. If only he could magically prolong her sleep, open her relaxed arms and kiss her transparent lids, blue-tinged by the hidden black of her eyes.

Lying once again in the hollow of the warm bed, Antoine, his jangled nerves soothed, continued his pleasurable fantasies. Now that the first daylight was coming, grey and re-assuring, he was going to close his eyes and possess the sleeping Minne at leisure. Minne was the youngest and slimmest of his habitual harem from which he sometimes selected Célénie, the plump, dark housemaid, the short-haired Polaire, Mademoiselle Moutardot who was queen of the Saint-Ambroise laundry, and Dido who was queen of Carthage.

Antoine and Minne, alone in the echoing dining-room, were standing by the closed window, eating their mid-afternoon snack and gloomily watching the rain fall. It was fine, close rain, scurrying eastward in drifting veils that swayed in the wind like the skirts of a gauze dress. Antoine was appeasing his hunger with a long, thick slice of currant bread in which his teeth left half-moons. Minne, her little finger in the air, was holding a thinner slice which she had forgotten to eat in the endeavour to find something unknown far away, through the rain, beyond the round mountains. Because of the cold rain, Minne had reverted to her straight, high-waisted green velvet frock with the white muslin bertha that followed the drooping line of her shoulders. Antoine liked that frock which made Minne look six months younger but it reminded him ruefully that school started again in October.

Only another month and he would have to leave Minne, this fantastic Minne who said monstrous things with a calm air of not understanding them, accused people of murder and rape, who offered her velvety cheek and repulsed the kiss with eyes full of hatred. He was devoted to this Minne with all his heart, as a schoolboy Don Juan, as a protective brother, as a timid lover, sometimes even as a father ... as for example on the day when she had cut herself with a penknife and clenched her lips and looked fierce to keep back the tears. The memory of that sad day made his heart swell with a tenderness which shamed him in his own eyes. He stretched out his long arms and slid a glance at his fair-haired Minne whose mind was so far away. Wanting to cry, wanting to hug her, he exclaimed:

'Filthy weather!'

At last Minne averted her gaze from the ashen horizon and stared at him, in silence. For no reason, he lost his temper.

'What do you mean by staring at me like that as if you knew something bad about me?'

She sighed, holding her bitten slice of bread and butter between her fingertips.

'I'm not hungry.'

'Good Lord! But Célénie's currant bread is marvellous!'

Minne wrinkled her elegant nose.

'So it seems! You eat like a bricklayer.'

'And you peck like a sparrow!'

'I don't feel like currant bread today.'

'What *do* you feel like? Fresh butter on hot rolls? Cream cheese?'

'No. I'd like a stick of pink rock.'

'Aunt wouldn't approve,' said Antoine, expressing no further surprise. 'And besides, it isn't nice.'

'Oh yes it is! A stick of pink rock that's a bit stale, when the top's gone white and a little soft and there's nothing left in the middle but a little tube of hard sugar that cracks like glass ... Take my slice of bread and put it on the sideboard: it irritates me.'

He obeyed and came back and sat on a low chair at Minne's feet.

'Talk to me, Antoine. You're my friend, amuse me!'

It was just as he feared. The dignity of being a friend reduced Antoine to extreme embarrassment. When Minne told stories of murder or outrages against morality, all went well; but he declared himself incapable of talking all on his own.

'And, besides, Minne, you realize that a young man like me doesn't have a repertoire of stories suitable for young girls!'

'Well, and what about *me*?' retorted Minne, hurt. 'Do you imagine I could tell you everything that goes on in my class? Why, half those prim and proper girls who come to the class could teach old Luzeau a thing or two!'

'You don't say!'

'I certainly do say. And the proof is that five or six of them have lovers.'

'You're joking! Their families would know.'

'Not at all, Sir! They're too cunning.'

'And how do *you* know?'

'I've got eyes, haven't I?'

Ah, she certainly had eyes! Terribly serious eyes which she bent on Antoine in a way that nearly made him giddy.

'Yes, you've got eyes. But so have their parents! Where do your girl-friends meet their lovers?'

'When they come out of class, of course,' replied Minne, unshaken. 'They exchange letters.'

'That's a good one! If they only exchange letters!'

'What are you laughing at?'

'Well, your girl-friends don't run the risk of getting landed with a baby!'

Minne fluttered her lashes, mistrustful of her incomplete knowledge.

'I'm only saying what I choose to say. Do you think I'm going to expose the élite of Parisian society to ... to shame and dishonour?'

'Minne, you talk like a novelette!'

'And *you* talk like a guttersnipe!'

'Minne, you have a horrible nature!'

'Oh, I have, have I? Then I'll go.'

'All right then, go!'

She turned away with great dignity and was about to leave the room when a sudden ray of sunshine bursting between the clouds made both children exclaim 'Ah!' with the same joyful surprise. The sun! What luck! The fingered shadows of the chestnut leaves were dancing on the parquet floor at their feet.

'Come on, Antoine! Let's run!'

She ran out into the still dripping garden, followed by Antoine, trailing sulkily behind her. She ran along the still soaking paths, gazing at the rejuvenated garden. In the distance, the ridge of the mountains steamed like the back of an overdriven horse and the earth was drinking in the last drops in a pullulating silence.

In front of the Venetian Sumac, known in France as a 'peruque tree', Minne stopped dead, dazzled. It was as rosy and ornate and vaporous as the sky on a Trianon ceiling. The dappled clouds of its hair sparkled with diamond raindrops; she would not have been surprised to see naked Cupids, the kind that hold festoons of blue ribbon and have too much vermilion on their cheeks and behinds, fly up out of it.

The espalier was dripping, but the lemon-shaped peaches known as 'Venus's breasts' had stayed warm and dry under their painted waterproof velvet. The roses were heavy with rain, and so that she could shake them, Minne had turned back her sleeves, displaying slim ivory arms, iridescent with a down even paler than her hair. Antoine watched her morosely, biting his lips at the thought that he could kiss those arms, feel that silver down caress his mouth.

Now she was squatting down over a red slug, the delicate tips of her curls trailing in a puddle.

'Look, Antoine, how red and grainy it is – just like a leather handbag.'

He did not deign to bend his head and his big nose remained sulkily stuck in the air.

'Antoine, please turn it over. I want to see if it'll be fine tomorrow.'

'How?'

'It was Célénie who told me: if slugs have earth on the end of their noses, it's a sign of fine weather.'

'Turn it over yourself!'

'No, slugs are disgusting.'

Grumbling, so as to preserve his dignity, Antoine turned the slug over with a twig. It dribbled and contracted itself. Minne was very attentive.

'Which end is its nose?'

Squatting beside her, Antoine could not prevent his eyes from glancing towards Minne's ankles under the white frilled petticoat and up to the embroidered scallops on her little white knickers. The shameless animal in him quivered with excitement: he thought that a sudden push would throw Minne on her back in the wet path. But she leapt to her feet with one bound.

'Come on, Antoine! We're going to collect berries under the dogwood tree!'

Pink with animation, she dragged him off to the rain-washed, grateful kitchen garden. The hollow, metallic leaves of the cabbages were brimming over with jewels and the delicate red-berried asparagus fern shimmered with a glittering frost.

'Minne! A striped snail! Look – it's just like a peppermint humbug!'

> Snail, snail, show me your horns!
> If you won't show them, beware!
> Your mother and father will beat you
> And the King of France will eat you!

Minne sang the old nursery rhyme in her high pure voice, then suddenly interrupted herself.

'A *double* snail, Antoine!'

'What d'you mean, double?'

He bent down and looked sheepish, not daring to touch the two coupled snails or to look at Minne, who was bending down too.

'Don't touch, Minne! It's dirty!'

'Why dirty? No dirtier than an almond or a hazel-nut. It's a filippino snail!'

After this tremendous rain, the heat had returned with almost unbearable fierceness, and The Dry House had closed its shutters again.

Mamma, in her light cotton frocks, complained: 'Life has become impossible!' Uncle Paul killed the slow hours of the day in his bedroom and the dark dining-room, full of echoes and creakings, once again sheltered a languid Minne and a blissful Antoine. He was sitting opposite his cousin and lazily setting out the thirteen heaps of cards of a patience. He was enchanted to have a changed Minne in front of him, a Minne who had boldly put up her hair in a high chignon, 'so as to be cool'. When she turned her head, she revealed a nape, a little bluish, like a lily in shadow, on which ethereal strands of hair, escaped from the chignon, curled in delicious tendrils.

Under this coiffure which disguised her as a 'grown-up lady', Minne's face wore a politely sarcastic expression which showed that she was far from impressed by Antoine and his attempt at sartorial elegance: white duck trousers, tussore shirt, broad belt buckled tight. Without his suspecting it, his red silk shirt, his black hair and his sunburnt skin made him look terribly like a cowboy in a circus. For the first time, Antoine realized the inadequacy of efforts to make oneself attractive and that a lover cannot be handsome if he is not loved.

Minne got up and muddled the cards.

'That's enough! It's too hot!'

She went over to the closed shutters, applied her eye to a round worm-hole and watched the spectacle of the heat as if it were a storm.

'If you could only see! There's not a leaf moving. And the kitchen cat! He's mad to roast himself like that! He'll get sun-stroke, he looks flat out as it is. I tell you I can feel the heat getting into my eye through the hole in the shutter!'

She turned back into the room, waving her arms 'to make a breeze' and asked:

'What shall we do?'

'I don't know. Read?'

'No, it keeps one hot.'

Antoine examined Minne from head to foot. How slim she was in her transparent frock!

'A dress like that can't weigh much!'

'It still feels too heavy. Though I've got almost nothing on underneath. Look . . .'

She lifted the hem of her dress a little between her thumb and finger, like a skirt-dancer. Antoine had a glimpse of brown lisle stockings which had openwork over the pearly ankles and little lace-edged drawers, fitting tight above the knees. The patience cards slipped out of his trembling hands and fell on the floor.

'I shan't be such a fool as the last time,' he thought wildly.

He swallowed a great mouthful of saliva and managed to feign indifference.

'That's down below. But perhaps you're hot up above, under the top of your dress?'

'All I've got under that is my bra and my chemise ... feel!'

She presented her back, with her head turned towards him, her elbows raised and her chest thrown out. He thrust out his hands, hurriedly searching for the almost flat side of the little breasts. Minne, who he had barely touched, jumped away from him with a squeak like a mouse and burst into spasms of laughter that brought tears to her eyes.

'Idiot! Idiot! Oh, that's strictly forbidden! Don't ever touch me under the arms! I think I'd have hysterics!'

She was giggling with sheer nerves, but he thought she was being provocative. Besides, he had just caught a scent from her moist armpits that went to his head. He had a frantic desire to touch Minne's skin, the secret skin that never saw daylight, to pull open her white underclothes as one pulls open the petals of a rose – oh! not to do her any harm, only to see. He forced himself to be gentle, feeling his hands all at once extraordinarily clumsy and powerful.

'Don't laugh so loud,' he whispered, advancing on her.

She gradually calmed down, still laughing and twitching her shoulders, and dried her eyes with her fingertips.

'Have a heart! I can't stop myself. For mercy's sake, don't start again! ... No, Antoine, or I'll scream!'

'Don't scream,' he implored, very low.

But, as he continued to advance, Minne retreated, her elbows pressed close to her sides to safeguard the ticklish place. Soon she was driven back against the door. Buttressing herself against it, she stretched out two threatening, pleading hands. Antoine seized her slender wrists and forced her timorous arms apart, thinking, when he had done so, how useful two extra hands would be at this moment for he dared not let go of Minne's wrists. She stood there, silent and uncertain, and he could see her eyes shifting uneasily, like troubled pools.

Stray strands of her hair tickled Antoine's chin and set up a furious itching which ran all over his body like a flame. To appease, without letting go of Minne's wrists, he pushed her arms further apart, plastered himself against her and rubbed his body against hers like a young, ignorant, excited dog.

A snake-like writhing repulsed him; the slender wrists turned and twisted in his fingers like the necks of strangled swans.

'You brute! You brute! Let go of me!'

He recoiled with a bound against the window and Minne remained against the door as if she were nailed to it; a white seagull with black, restless eyes.

She had not really understood. She had felt herself in danger. The whole body of a boy had pressed so hard against hers that she could still feel its hard muscles and its bruising bones. A belated anger flared up in her, she wanted to burst into furious abuse. Instead she burst into great, scalding tears which she hid in her upturned apron.

'Minne!'

Antoine, stupefied, watched her crying, tormented with grief and remorse and also with the fear that Mamma might come back.

'Minne, please, *please* stop crying!'

'Yes,' she sobbed. 'I'll tell . . . I'll tell.'

Antoine flung his handkerchief on the floor in a fury.

'Oh, of course! "I'll tell Mamma all about it!" Girls are all the same, all they can do is tell tales. You're no better than the rest.'

Instantly, Minne uncovered an offended face, dripping with tears and tumbled strands of hair.

'Oh, so that's what you think? Oh, so all I can do is tell tales? Oh, so I don't know how to keep secrets, don't I?

There are girls, let me tell you, who are bullied and insulted . . .'

'Minne!'

'. . . And who have more loads on their minds than all the schoolboys in the world!'

That innocent word 'schoolboy' stung Antoine on the raw. Schoolboy! It summed up everything: the awkward age when one's sleeves are too short and one's moustache not long enough, when one's heart dilates at a scent or the rustle of a skirt – all the melancholic, feverish years of waiting. The sudden rage that flamed up in Antoine freed him from his fuddled intoxication: Mamma could safely come in now. She would find boy cousin and girl cousin standing confronting each other, measuring each other up with that drawing-in of the neck common to fighting cocks and fighting children. Minne was ruffling herself up like a white hen, her chignon in wild disarray, her muslin frock crumpled: Antoine, drenched with perspiration, was rolling up his red silk sleeves in the most unchivalrous manner. And then Mamma appeared, a referee in a light cotton dress, bearing two plates of yellow plums . . .

That night, Minne stood dreaming in her bedroom before getting undressed. Slowly she wound the last of her ringlets round a white ribbon and then stood motionless, her wide-open eyes fixed unseeing on the flame of the little lamp. With all her hair rolled up, tied with white ribbons into six golden snails, two on her forehead, two over her ears, and two on the nape of her neck, she looked like a tightly-crimped village girl.

The closed shutters imprisoned the oppressive air, and one could distinctly hear the woodworm boring a precious hole in their thickness. If they were opened, the mosquitoes would rush towards the lamp, sing in Minne's ears, as she leapt about like a goat, and marble her delicate cheeks with pink, swollen bites.

Minne went on dreaming instead of undressing; her mouth pensive, her black eyes, which mirrored a tiny image

55

of the lamp, fixed in a stare; beautiful, somnambulistic eyes under velvety blonde eyebrows whose noble curve lent so much seriousness to the childish face.

Minne was thinking of Antoine, of the madness that had suddenly made him tremble all over and turn so brutal. She had no idea how the struggle might have ended, but she had felt a dull rancour against him for being at that moment her schoolboy cousin Antoine and not someone else. Alone with herself, she felt as resentful towards him as if he had been some unknown man whom she had embraced, by mistake, in the dark. There was not a trace of pity, even physical pity, for the poor ardent, clumsy boy. Minne protested with her whole being against a case of mistaken identity. For if the nonchalant sleeper of the Boulevard Berthier had suddenly sprung wide awake, seized her wrists in moist hands and strained a supple body, that smelt of lazy flesh and warm sand, against hers, Minne trembled at the presentiment that such an assault, reinforced with gentle gestures and insolent looks, would have found her submissive and hardly even surprised.

'I must go on waiting and waiting,' she thought obstinately. 'He'll escape from his prison and come back to wait for me at the corner of the Avenue Gourgaud. Then I'll go away with him. He'll present me to his people as their queen, he'll kiss me – on the mouth – in front of all of them, while they mutter with envy. Our love will grow greater in the daily peril.'

The Dry House creaked. Outside, with a rustle as light as a trailing dress, a warm wind swept away the fallen flowers of the trumpet-creeper.

'More ridiculous things have been known,' Antoine assured himself, doodling ink-dots on his desk and biting his cherry-wood penholder. The Latin composition made him feel almost physically sick; he was prematurely experiencing that sinking feeling of term beginning again which makes schoolboys turn pale on the first morning of October. The nearer the end of September approached, the more Antoine's soul turned desperately to Minne; white and golden Minne, Minne the refreshing image of a free July, of a beautiful new month, as bright and shining as a virgin coin. Minne, as fleeting and elusive as time itself, Minne and the holidays! . . . Oh! to keep Minne for ever, to sharpen his wits little by little by pitting them against her deep duplicity under that mask of candour. There was indeed a way, an arrangement, a brilliant and natural solution . . . 'More ridiculous things have been known,' he told himself for the twentieth time, 'than long engagements between a boy of eighteen and a girl of fifteen. In royal families, for instance . . .' But what was the point of arguing? Minne would or she wouldn't and that was all. A little golden-haired girl had only to nod or shake her head and the whole world could be changed.

It struck eleven. Antoine got up, tragic as if the Louis-Philippe clock were striking his last hour. The glass on the mantelpiece showed him the image of a tall, resolute daredevil with an adventurous nose whose eyes, under the shelter of the bushy eyebrows, said: 'Conquer or die!' He crossed the passage and knocked peremptorily on Minne's door. She was all alone, sitting on a chair, and frowning a little because Antoine had banged the door.

'Minne?'

'What?'

She had said only one word. But that word implied so many nasty sarcastic things, such defiance, such exaggerated politeness . . . The valiant Antoine did not weaken.

'Minne! Minne . . . do you love me?'

Accustomed to the illogical behaviour of this savage, Minne looked at him sideways, without turning her head. He repeated:

'Minne, do you love me?'

An indescribable expression of irony, casual pity and uneasiness flickered in the dark eye that had slid into one corner under the fair lashes; the nervous mouth twitched in a fleeting smile. In a second, Minne had resumed her defensive armour.

'Am I fond of you? Of course I am.'

'I didn't ask you if you were fond of me. I asked you if you loved me.'

The black eye had turned away. Minne was staring at the window and displaying only a profile whose lines melted into the golden light that made it seem almost ethereal.

'Pay attention, Minne. I want to say something very serious to you. And what you answer is something very serious too. Minne, do you love me enough to marry me later on?'

This time, she turned to face him. Antoine found himself confronted with a kind of stubborn angel whose menacing eyes had already answered before her voice said:

'No.'

At first he did not feel the physical pain he had anticipated, the pain that would have prevented him from thinking. He only had the sensation that his skull had burst and let in water that flooded his brain. But he kept his countenance.

'Is that your answer?'

Minne considered it unnecessary to repeat it. With her head bent, she surreptitiously studied Antoine. One of his feet was thrust forward, almost imperceptibly tapping the floor.

'Minne, is it indiscreet to ask your reason for saying no?'

She sighed, expelling a long breath that made stray hairs on her cheek flutter up like feathers. Pensively she bit her little finger, gazed in a friendly way at the unhappy Antoine, who, stiff as a soldier on parade, was stoically letting the sweat trickle all down his temples, and at last deigned to reply:

'Because I'm engaged.'

She was engaged. That was all Antoine had been able to get out of her. All questions had died on his lips, confronted with those unfathomable eyes and that mouth tightly closed on a secret or a lie. Alone once again in his bedroom, Antoine clutched his hair and tried to think clearly.

She had lied. Or else she hadn't lied. He did not know

which of the two alternatives was the worst. 'Girls are awful!' he thought ingenuously. Scraps of novels passed in actual print before his eyes. 'The cruelty of woman ... the duplicity of woman ... feminine unscrupulousness ...' 'Perhaps they suffered, the men who wrote that,' he thought with sudden pity. 'But at least their suffering is over and mine is only beginning. Suppose I went and asked my aunt the truth?' He knew very well that he would not go, and it was not only shyness that stopped him, it was that everything coming from Minne was sacred. Confidences, lies, admissions: all Minne's precious words to Antoine must be locked up inside him, an inestimable treasure that he would guard against all.

'Minne is engaged!' he repeated those three words over to himself with a respectful despair, as if his fair-haired Minne had achieved some remarkable distinction; almost as he might have said: 'Minne is a major in the army,' or 'Minne is top in Greek prose.' It was not this sincere lover's fault that he was only eighteen.

It was a pitiful body that writhed, half-undressed, on Antoine's bed. The poor boy, as he heaved great grunting sighs like a man hewing down a tree, was labouring to understand something: that sorrow can inflame the senses and that it would doubtless be a long time before he was mature enough to be able to suffer purely.

Minne was ill. The house was in a silent bustle: Mamma's eyes were red in her drawn face. Uncle Paul had talked of puberal fever, of going through a difficult time, of a gastric upset. Mamma was out of her wits. Her darling, her little ray of sunshine, her white chicken had a temperature and had been in bed for two days.

Antoine wandered about, ready to accuse himself of everything that had happened. He slipped his long nose round the half-open door of Minne's bedroom, but his big shoes creaked and he was shushed away and driven back downstairs. He had only caught the merest glimpse of Minne lying, pale, in the blue and green chintz bed.

She drank a little milk – a very little – making a faint noise with her dry lips, then fell back and sighed. Apart from the mauve rings round her eyes and that crease at the corner of her delicate nostrils, she might have taken to her bed for a whim. Only, at night, when Mamma had drawn the curtains and lit the nightlight in the blue glass, there was a change. Minne would sigh more loudly, wave her hands about, sit up, lie down again and begin to mutter indistinct words: 'He's asleep ... he's pretending to be asleep ... the queen ... Queen Minne;' short, babyish sentences like a child talking in its sleep.

One misty red dawn, which smelt of damp moss and mushrooms and smoke, Minne woke and announced that she felt better. Before Mamma could believe her joy, Minne yawned, showed a rather pale but clean tongue, stretched out every limb to its utmost in bed and asked a hundred questions: 'What time is it? Where's Antoine? Is it fine? Can I have some chocolate?'

Two days later, she sipped an egg beaten up in milk to the last drop. Minne, feeling greedy and propped up comfortably between two pillows, was enjoying the rôle of convalescent. The delicious breeze, through the open window, swelled the curtains and made her think of the sea.

Tomorrow, Minne would get up. Today it was damp and the leaves were showering down. The west wind sang under the doors with a wintry voice, a voice that made one want to roast chestnuts in the ashes. Minne was clutching a big white woollen shawl round her shoulders and her plaited hair revealed her rosy porcelain ears. She had allowed Antoine to come in to keep her company and he showed the discreet gratitude of a lost dog who has been found. Minne's sharpened chin moved him almost to tears; he wanted to take this child in his arms and lull her to sleep. Why did he have to read in the mysterious dark eyes so much malice and so little trust? He had already read aloud, talked about the weather, his father's health and their approaching departure and still that penetrating gaze did not soften. He was about to resume the novel he had begun to read aloud, but a tapering hand stretched out of the bed and stopped him.

'Don't read any more,' begged Minne. 'It tires me.'

'Do you want me to go?'

'No ... Antoine, listen! The only person I trust here is you. You can do me a great favour.'

'Yes?'

'I want you to write a letter for me. A letter Mamma mustn't see. If Mamma saw me writing in bed she might ask who I was writing to. If *you're* sitting at that table, writing, you're keeping me company and no one will see anything odd about it. I want to write to my fiancé.'

Having dealt him this blow, she could have scrutinized her cousin's face as much as she liked. Antoine had made great headway in self-control and he did not flinch. By living close to Minne he had acquired the sense of the extraordinary and unpredictable. An idea, as simple as Minne's ferocity, had shot through his mind: 'I shall write without letting her see a thing; then I'll know who *he* is and I'll kill him.'

Without a word, he meekly followed Minne's instructions.

'In my blotter ... No, not that paper ... white paper without the address on it. We're obliged to take precautions, he and I!'

When he was seated and he had moistened the new nib with his tongue and settled the blotting-pad firmly, she dictated:

'My beloved ...'

He did not start. Neither did he write. He looked long and probingly at Minne, without anger, until she became impatient.

'Well, go on! Write!'

'Minne,' said Antoine in a low, altered voice: 'Why are you doing this?'

She crossed her white shawl over her chest, in a gesture of defiance. A new emotion flushed her transparent cheeks. Antoine seemed strange to her and it was her turn to stare at him with a far-away prophetic gaze. Was she perhaps discovering, through him, a momentary regret for the Antoine he would be in five or six years; tall, robust, as much at ease in his skin as in a suit made to measure, having kept nothing of what he was today but those gentle eyes that gave him the air of a kindly, black-haired brigand?

'Why, Minne? Why are you doing this to me?'

'Because you're the only person I trust.'

Trust! She had found the one word that was enough to shatter Antoine's resolution. He would obey, he would write the letter, swept on by the flood of that sublime cowardice that has absolved so many complaisant husbands, so many humble lovers who have to share their loves.

'My beloved, your dear eyes must not be surprised to see a handwriting that is not mine. I am ill and someone devoted to me ...'

Minne's voice hesitated as if she were translating a difficult text word by word.

'Someone devoted to me . . . wants to write to you and give you news of me so as to reassure you, so that you can give yourself wholly to your dangerous career . . .'

'His dangerous career!' ruminated Antoine. 'Is he a fireman? Or a lion-tamer in a circus?'

'Have you got that, Antoine? . . . your dangerous career. My beloved . . . when shall I be once more in your arms and breathe your dear smell?'

A great wave of bitterness swept through the heart of the one who was writing. He was enduring all this like some painful dream in which one suffers agonies while knowing that it is a dream.

'Your dear smell. Sometimes I would like to forget that I have been yours. Have you got that, Antoine?'

He had not got it. He turned a face towards her that was like a drowning man's, a face distorted and ugly with the effort not to choke. Minne was promptly irritated.

'Oh, for goodness' sake, get on!'

He did not get on. He shook his head as if to chase away a fly.

'You're not telling the truth,' he said at last. 'Or else you're going out of your mind. You haven't ever given yourself to a man.'

Nothing exasperated Minne more than incredulity. She drew her concealed legs up under her with an abrupt grace. The luminous black eyes opened wide and overwhelmed Antoine with their anger.

'I *have*!' she cried. 'I *have* given myself to him!'

'No!'

'*Yes!*'

'No!'

'*Yes* . . .'

And she hurled at him, like an unanswerable argument:

'Of course I have! Since he's my lover!'

The effect of such a categorical word on Antoine was, to say the least of it, surprising. All his tense, obstinate attitude relaxed. He laid his pen carefully down beside the ink-pot, got up without overturning his chair and walked over to the

bed. Minne trembled. All she was aware of was that Antoine's eyes gleamed with the strange, savage gentleness of a
beast about to spring.

'You have a lover? You've slept with him?' he asked very
low, his voice dwelling almost melodiously on the last
words.

Minne's bright flush seemed to him to admit her guilt.

'Certainly, I've slept with him!'

'Yes? Where, then?'

By a reversal of rôles which she did not notice, it was
now an embarrassed Minne who was replying to an aggressive Antoine imbued with a lucidity for which she was totally
unprepared.

'Where? Does that interest you?'

'It does interest me.'

'Very well then! At night ... on the bank of the
fortifications.'

He considered this, scrutinizing Minne with cautious,
screwed-up eyes.

'At night ... on the bank. You used to go out of the house?
Your mother knows nothing about it? No, I mean: is it
someone whose presence in the house you couldn't explain to
your mother?'

She nodded gravely.

'Someone ... inferior?'

'Inferior!'

Sitting bolt upright again and trembling with indignation,
her wide-open dark eyes flashed lightning at him, her
narrow, patrician little nostrils quivered. 'Inferior!' Inferior,
that silent, menacing lover whose supple body was flung
across the pavement in a graceful imitation of death! Narcissus in a striped jersey, lying in a swoon on the margin of a
spring. Inferior, the hero of so many nights, who hid the
still-warm knife under his clothes and bore the red marks of
so many terrified nails!

'I apologize, Minne,' said Antoine very gently. 'But ...
you talk of a dangerous career. What does he do then, your
... your friend?'

'I can't tell you.'

'A dangerous career ...' went on Antoine, patiently and warily. 'There are so many dangerous careers. He might be a roof-tiler ... or a bus-driver.'

She fixed a deadly gaze on him.

'You want to know what he does?'

'Yes, I'd rather ...'

'He's an assassin.'

Antoine raised his Mephistophelean eyebrows, gazed at her and burst into roars of boyish laughter. This huge joke completely restored him. He slapped his thighs with inelegant heartiness.

Minne shuddered: there flashed in her eyes, which reflected a red September sunset, a distinct longing to kill Antoine.

'You don't believe me?'

'Yes, of course ... of course! Oh, Minne, what a crazy girl you are!'

Minne was past all reason and patience.

'You don't believe me? And suppose I showed you him! Suppose I showed you him alive? He's handsome, much handsomer than you'll ever be, he's got a red and blue jersey and a black and purple check cap, and hands softer than a woman's. Every night he kills hideous old women who hide money in their mattresses and revolting old men who look like old Corne! He's head of a terrible gang that terrorizes Levallois-Perret. He waits for me at night at the corner of the Avenue Gourgaud.'

She stopped, out of breath, seeking for a final shaft to drive home:

'He waits for me there and when Mamma's gone to bed I go out and meet him and we spend the night together!'

She had reached the end of her tether. She lay back on the pillows, waiting for Antoine to burst out laughing. But his only reaction was a restrained anxiety, the fear that he had sent Minne's temperature up again and made her slightly delirious.

'I'm going, Minne.'

She closed her eyes, suddenly pale and sobered.

'All right, go!'

'Minne, you're not angry with me?'

She signified, 'No, no' with a weary shake of her head.

He raised a dry, hot, limp little hand from the sheet, hesitated to kiss it and gently – very gently – replaced it as if it were a delicate object he did not know how to use.

Some Sundays had passed since Minnie had left the Dry House, bringing Uncle Paul and Antoine back to gather round the traditional fruit tart. Minne rudely averted her eyes from them because the sight of Uncle Paul, yellow, shrivelled, offended her fresh, cruel youth and because Antoine, in his black uniform with the gilt buttons had resumed his old awkwardness and looked like a sun-baked overgrown boy from a military orphanage.

Minne had returned to her daily classes and no longer even looked out, at the corner of the deserted avenue, for the unknown man who filled all her thoughts. The pavement glistened with showers or rang under one's heels as on frosty December mornings. At night, Mamma embroidered under the lamp, turning round now and then to scrutinize her darling's face with the innocence of a fond, blind mother and then relapsing into her industrious peace. It was not Mamma's fault if God had endowed her with the gift of love, but not of discernment. Many an honest hen has hatched out a beautiful free-soaring wild duck under her own clipped wings.

'It's Him! It's Him!'

Minne, leaning so far over that she nearly fell out, clutched the window-sill with two hands that had gone cold with excitement. Her eyes, her heart, recognized him through the darkness.

'No one else but Him could walk like that! How supple he is! You can see his hips swaying at every step. He seems to have got thinner in prison. Is that the same black and purple check cap? He's waiting for me! He's come back! I want to show myself. He's going away. No! He's coming back!'

The man who was strolling along, smoking, was a tall loafer, so supple that he seemed boneless. The brightness of an open window, at this time of night, startled him; he looked up. Minne, full of crazy ideas, could have sworn that she recognized a pallor unlike anyone else's on that uplifted face and the smoke of that cigarette rose up to her like incense. She clicked her tongue.

'Psst!'

The man swerved round with a suddenness that betrayed an animal always on the watch. Was it that kid up there? What was the matter with her?

A light little voice asked:

'Have you come to fetch me? Shall I come down?'

On the off-chance, because the shape up there was young and slender, the man replied with a mocking and obscene gesture of his hands. 'Of course, it's the sign!' Minne told herself. 'But I can't go down like this.'

Feverishly, she began to deck herself out again in the fantastic array of last year – the red ribbon round the neck, the chignon – oh! that comb that kept slipping all the time! Should she take a coat? No; people aren't cold when they love each other. Hurry down!

Minne's feet, shod in red bedroom slippers, bounded downstairs, hardly touching the carpet. There was a terrible creak. Minne, in her haste, had forgotten the loose eighteenth step which groaned like a rusty door. She flattened herself against the wall and held her breath. Nothing in the house had stirred. Down below, the safety locks yielded to her small, groping hand: the front door opened silently – but how could she shut it again without making a noise?

'All right, I won't shut it!'

It was chilly, almost cold. The wind, which had already blown the last leaves off the plane-trees, made the gas-flames in the street lamps flicker.

'Where is he?'

No one in the avenue. Which way to go? Minne stood still, childishly wringing her bare hands in despair. Ah! over there a figure was moving away.

'Yes, yes, it's him!'

With one hand on her toppling chignon and the other holding her light skirt, she dashed forward. The unaccustomed hour and the seriousness of what she was doing carried her along on feet that hardly touched the ground. She could have spread out her arms and flown without feeling any more surprise. 'It's my soul that's running' was all she thought. She must run, and run very fast, for the tall figure of the man she was pursuing was no longer more than a swaying spectre going in the direction of the Porte Malesherbes.

Minne passed the Avenue Gourgaud, reached the gate of the railway and the Boulevard Malesherbes. With Célénie or Mamma, she had never gone further than this. The boulevard continued, with trees at intervals. Heavens, wherever had Curly gone? She dared not shout and she did not know how to whistle. There he was, over there! No, it was only a bigger tree! Ah, *there* he was! Having stopped for a moment to control her breathless excitement, she set off again and ran up to someone who seemed to be waiting; a silent man, the top of whose unknown face was hidden under the soft brim of a felt hat.

'Excuse me, Sir . . .'

The small, choked voice could hardly speak. All that could be seen of the man, under the greenish light of the gaslamp, was a chin blue with a three-days' beard. No forehead, no eyes, even the hands thrust into the pockets remained invisible. But Minne was not afraid of this faceless dummy which seemed as tall and hollow as an ancient suit of armour.

'You haven't seen a . . . a man go by who was going *that* way – a tall man, who sways a little as he walks?'

The man's shoulders rose and fell. Minne could feel an invisible gaze fixed on her and became impatient.

'But he must have passed by you.'

Her obstinate little face boldly searched the shadowy one. Running had flushed her cheeks, her eyes reflected the gasjet like two pools; she opened and shut her mouth and stamped her feet, waiting for an answer. The hollow man shrugged his shoulders again and finally said in a dull voice:

'No one did.'

She shook her head furiously and set off again faster, maddened at having lost time and ready to burst into tears with anguish.

It was darker on this side. But the gentle slope was good for running on and she ran and ran, thinking only about holding up her chignon which was bothering her. Without noticing she ran full tilt into a peaceful couple of policemen who were walking back up the boulevard. The sudden impact of a square shoulder made her stagger; she heard someone say gruffly:

'What's that damn little fool think she's doing?'

She ran on and on, the wind whistling in her ears. She ran straight ahead: Curly could only have followed the line of the fortifications which, for him, was a disputed kingdom, a far from safe refuge. At the bottom of the railway cutting, a train crawled along, enveloping her in a cloud of smoke as it passed her. She slowed down her tired feet, looked down and examined her slippers, whose pointed toes were already covered with mud, then leant against the gate to follow the red eye on the train. 'Where am I?'

Fifty yards further on, a bay of shadow blocked the road, a black cavern, over the top of which a long, living monster, plumed with smoke and perforated with holes of red and yellow fire, was passing.

'Another train! It's going over the boulevard. I didn't know of this bridge. If it's one of their refuges, *he's* waiting for me there!'

She ran on, her lips trembling. Her decisions followed each other so swiftly and inevitably that it was impossible for her not to realize that she was guided by the second sight that only love can give. Her hand, clutching the top of her chignon, seemed to be lifting her whole body up and holding it by three frail fingers; the wind blew down her throat, drying it.

The black mouth of the tunnel under the bridge, which yawned wider as she approached, did not frighten her. She felt herself on the threshold of another life, on the verge of initiation into sacred mysteries. Strands of hair, that had come undone and escaped from her tortoise-shell comb, streamed out behind her or fell back on the nape of her neck, fluttering like living feathers. Something had stirred, something blacker than the reddish gloom, something seated on the ground under the halo of iridescent fog that circled the gas-jet. Was it he? No! A squatting woman, two women, and a very short, puny man. Minne's silent feet had not warned them of her approach and, in any case, the bridge was still vibrating with a dull rumble.

She ran on, straining her eyes to try and make out the figure of the man she was pursuing. He was not there. These people were of his kind, perhaps his subjects. The man – a kind of stunted child – seated on the pavement sported the well-known jersey and the soft cloth cap glued to the skull. Behind the group, a forest of fluted pillars disappeared into the darkness.

Entirely hidden in the shadow of a pillar, Minne thought:

'It's like Pompeii.'

One of the two women had just got up; she wore the typical apron and cheap, flashy blouse and her metallic black hair was piled up in a helmet-shaped chignon so smooth and tightly-strained that it gleamed like the carapace of a fighting insect. Minne stared avidly, comparing the woman with herself: what *she* lacked was that particular chic of a coiffure with not a single hair out of place and that red woollen blouse, fastened at the neck with a butterfly bow of coarse lace. Above all, it was that indescribable something in her bearing, at once aggressive and discouraged, something of the cynicism and the listlessness of an animal that lives, feeds, scratches itself and gratifies all its instincts out-of-doors. 'From now on, these are my people,' Minne told herself proudly. 'If I ask them, they'll tell me where Curly is waiting for me.'

The woman who had got up stretched out her masculine arms and gave a prodigious yawn; Minne could see a broad back, barred by the ridge of the corsets. Then she coughed convulsively and swore blasphemously in an exhausted voice.

'All the same, I must make up my mind,' Minne told herself firmly. Having fixed her chignon more securely, she thrust her hands in her heart-shaped pockets and emerged from her lair in the shadow. Standing with one foot thrust forward under her skirt, she inquired:

'Excuse me, ladies, you don't happen to have seen a tall man go by – a man who sways a little as he walks?'

She had spoken in a high, rapid voice like a little actress who has more zeal than experience. The two creatures with their backs glued to the wall stared stupidly at this child in fancy dress.

'Whatever's this?' asked the exhausted voice of the woman who had been coughing.

'It's a kid,' said the other. 'She doesn't half look a scream.'

Down below, the puny little man, hunched up like a frog, burst into fits of laughter, then said, in the nasal voice of a hunchback:

'Who you lookin' for, baby?'

Offended, Minne glanced down regally at the deformed little monster.

'I am looking for Curly.'

The freak stood up and ceremoniously removed his cap, revealing an almost bald head.

'*I'm* Curly, at your service.'

The two women laughed. Minne frowned and was about to pass on, but the tramp came closer and whispered confidentially:

'I've got curly hair but it can only be seen in private.'

Then, as his hand stole slyly towards Minne's waist, she shuddered in every nerve and fled. For a minute she was pursued by the shuffle of slipshod feet; then it was interrupted by the voices of the two women:

'Antonin! Antonin! Let her alone, I say!'

It was not fear that made Minne's heart pound and lent wings to her feet, but offended pride – the scalding humiliation of a queen embraced by a menial. 'They did not realize who I was! Unlucky for them, if they're my subjects later on! I'll tell him . . . but, oh heavens! where can I find him?'

She walked fast, already too tired to run. However long had she been walking on this road and this slope? How few people there were about tonight! Where were they all? Perhaps there was a great council being held in a quarry? She wanted to sit down on a bench to empty her slippers which were full of sand and sharp little pebbles. But an embraced couple which drew apart at her approach drove her away with words she couldn't understand.

A sudden 'Pssst!' attracted her attention and made her stop.

'Is it you?' she cried.

'Yes, it's me,' replied a voice in an assumed falsetto.

'Who are you?'

'Why *me*, of course. Your sweetheart, Prince Charming.'

'It's not you I'm looking for!' replied Minne severely.

She walked on again, drawing a little to one side to let a flock of sheep go by: little dry hooves pitting the soil, bleating in different keys, a peaceful, cheesy smell. Minne could hear the snuffling of the sheep-dogs as they ran to and fro and feel the round woolly rumps brush against her. They went by with a noise like a hail-storm and for a moment it seemed to Minne that they had carried all the sounds of the night away with them. But a train rumbled in the distance and then rushed furiously by, spitting out a shower of red cinders behind it.

Minne stopped walking and leant up against a tree. To combat her weariness, she told herself once more: 'I shall find him in the end, if I go on asking. It's my fault as well! I wasted time by wanting to make myself beautiful! Could he have thought that I doubted him? No, I didn't doubt him! I don't doubt him any more than I doubt myself!'

Standing up straight again and sweeping both hands over her silvery hair, she defied the darkness, for by now her eyes had had time to get used to it. She lifted up her painful feet and stared at her stiff cold hands in the light of a foggy gaslamp then, all alone as she was, she laughed; a sad, ironical little laugh.

'If Mamma were here, I know just what she'd say. "My little Minne, what's the good of my bothering to buy you white fur gloves?" But that's not what I'm worrying about. If only, at least, I had a brush or a rag to take the mud off my slippers! Fancy appearing before him with dirty feet!'

In search of a bit of grass to wipe her shoes, she crossed the deserted avenue. Then something made her start. She had not noticed a woman who was pacing up and down on the soft sand with the mournful step of an animal that knows it cannot get out of its cage. This woman wore the metallic helmet of hair, the cotton apron and shoes, adorned with rosettes, that were pathetically unsuitable for walking in puddles.

'Madame!' Minne called out resolutely, for the creature was moving away, jealous of her solitude, the solitude of a timid wild animal that hunts alone and is satisfied with small game. 'Madame!'

The woman turned round, but continued to move away backwards. She was a mannish, squarely built creature with a purplish face and suspicious little piglike eyes. Minne, who saw in her a slight resemblance to Célénie, resumed her most regal self-assurance and said in a high voice, with her dishevelled head in the air:

'Look, Madame, I've lost my way. Could you tell me the name of this avenue?'

A toneless voice, like the voice of farm dogs that sleep out-of-doors, replied, after a silence:

'It's written on the signs, isn't it?'

'I'm quite aware of that,' said Minne impertinently. 'But I don't know this neighbourhood at all. I'm looking for some-one . . . And someone I'm sure you know, Madame!'

'Someone I know?'

The mannish woman repeated Minne's last words in a thick speech in which lingered a faint trace of a country accent.

'I don't know many people.'

Minne meant to laugh, but coughed instead, because she was cold.

'You needn't keep things back from me! I'm one of you ... or I'm going to be!'

The woman, who kept her distance, appeared not to have understood. She raised her head towards the black sky, and said, for the sake of saying something:

'It'll rain before daylight.'

Minne stamped her foot. Rain! Inferior creature! Rain, wind, lightning, what did all that matter? There were only the hours of night and the hours of day. By day one sleeps, one smokes, one dreams. But, under the black velvet tent of the night, one kills, one loves, one rattles the golden coins still sticky with blood. Oh, to find Curly, to forget a childhood of slavery and passionately obey him and him only! Minne pawed the ground, snuffed the night air, fired once again with feverish enthusiasm.

'You look very young,' muttered that dull voice like a hoarse watch-dog's.

Minne gazed haughtily at the woman, between her lashes.

'Very young! I shall be sixteen in eight months' time.'

'Better hurry up and be. It's safer.'

'Ah!'

'D'you work all alone?'

'I don't work,' said Minne proudly. 'Others work for me.'

'You're mighty lucky. Are they your younger or older sisters?'

'I haven't got any sisters. And, besides, what has it got to do with you? If you'd only just tell me ... I'm looking for Curly. I have something to tell him, something extremely important.'

The sad monster had come closer to stare at this frail little girl, who talked as if she were quite at home here, who was got up like someone going to a fancy-dress ball, with her hair so dishevelled that it was a disgrace and was inquiring for 'Curly'.

'Curly? Which Curly then?'

'Why, *the* Curly, of course. The one who was with Copper-Nob, the head of the Aristos of Levallois-Perret.'

'The one who was with Copper-Nob? The one who ... D'you think I know those sort of people? Where did you get such ideas, you fucking little shit?'

'But ...'

'I'd have you know I'm a respectable woman, you dirty little bitch. No one's ever seen a pimp crawling under my skirt since the '89 Exhibition! It's got no more hair on its twat than I have on my hand and it talks of gangs and Curly and this and that and the other! Be off with you, will you? And look sharp about it, or there'll be precious little left of *your* curls by the time I've done with you!'

'What an unheard-of thing!'

Minne, out of breath, sat down on the edge of the pavement, free at last from the appalling pursuit of the termagant, who had rushed after her, with frog-like leaps and incomprehensible threats. Panic-stricken, Minne had dashed over to the other side of the boulevard, plunged into a little street, then into another until she reached this narrow, dark, deserted thoroughfare where the wind moaned as it did in the country and froze her damp shoulders. She clutched her elbows to her sides and coughed, as she tried to understand.

'Yes, it's extraordinary! Wherever I go, I'm treated as an enemy! There are too many things I can't make out. And I've been running for an awfully long time: I can't go any further.'

Her back was bowed with exhaustion; her head, with its dishevelled sheaf of hair, drooped down over her knees. For the first time since her flight, Minne remembered a warm bed and a pink and white bedroom. She was ashamed of being huddled there in a limp heap on the pavement, with her dress all muddy. She would have to begin all over again. She must go back home, hope that once again Curly would come, that once again she would feverishly adorn herself and escape ... Oh! if only that night would come, that night of fulfilment, brimming over with love! She longed for a strong, compulsive arm to guide her first steps, for an unerring hand to lift, one by one, all the veils that hid the unknown, for Minne felt exhausted to the point of sleep, to the point of death.

The silence and the cold awakened her. 'Where am I?' She came to from dozing for a few minutes on the edge of the pavement feeling utterly bewildered, cut off from the real world and with no idea what time it was – prepared to believe that a nightmare had transported her into one of those lands where even immovable objects take on an aspect of nameless terror.

What had become of the fierce Minne, the mistress of a notorious assassin, the queen of the red-handed people? She sat shivering like a thin little bird in her pink summer blouse, coughing and looking all about her with scared black eyes. Her chignon had come undone and her long fair hair hung down in a sadly dishevelled mass. Her mouth was trembling, too, with the effort to keep back the word which would allay all terrors, summon embracing arms, light and shelter: 'Mamma!' But Minne would not cry out that word unless she felt she were dying, unless terrifying beasts were carrying her off, unless her blood was pouring from her gashed throat ... That word was the last resource and it must not be used in vain!

She got up and courageously set off again, forcing her mind to dwell on sensible things:

'First of all, I must look at the name of the street, mustn't I? And then I shall find the way home, and then I'll go in very quietly, and then it'll all be over ...'

At the corner of the narrow, deserted alley she stood on tip-toe to read its name. 'I've never even heard of this street. Never mind, perhaps I'll recognize the next one.'

The next one was deserted too, bumpy with loose cobblestones and heaped with piles of filth. Another street, another, and another, all bearing odd, unfamiliar names ... Minne stood rooted to the spot, her hands dangling at her sides, feeling a crazy fear mounting up little by little: 'I've been transported into an unknown city while I was asleep! If I could even see a policeman. Yes, but ... Got up as I am, the first thing he'd do would be to take me to the station.'

She walked on again, sometimes stopping, with her head thrown back to read the street names, sometimes hesitating and retracing her steps in a desperate effort to find the way out of the labyrinth.

'If I sit down, I shall die here.'

This thought kept Minne going. Not that the idea of death frightened her but, little, lost, suffering animal that she was, she wanted to die in her lair.

The sharper cold, the rising wind and the slow distant rumbling of carts all indicated that it was nearly morning but Minne was quite unaware of this. She walked on, unconsciously; limping, because her feet were hurting and one of her red slippers had lost a heel. Suddenly she stopped and pricked up her ears: a step was approaching, tapping to the gay rhythm of someone humming a popular song.

It was a man. Or rather a 'gentleman'. Rather old and rather heavily built, he was walking towards her, bundled up in a fur-collared overcoat. Minne's spirits soared up again.

'How kind he looks! And how reassuring! How warm and soft his fur-lined coat must be! Oh, heavens, for some warmth! Just a little warmth! It seems so long since I had any!'

She was about to run up to the man, fling herself on him as on a grandfather, and sob out that she had got lost, that Mamma would know everything if she was not home before daylight ... But she controlled herself, with the prudence that comes of a long series of misfortunes: suppose the man did not believe her and chased her away? Standing in the fine rain that had begun to fall, Minne readjusted her damp hair as best she could, made a vain effort to smooth out the creases in her pink apron and tried to assume a very natural expression, no more embarrassed than one would expect in a young girl of good family who had lost her way when out for a walk.

'I shall say to him ... oh dear, he's nearly here! ... I shall say to him: "Excuse me, Sir, would you be kind enough to tell me the way to the Boulevard Berthier?" '

The man was so close that she could smell his cigar. She emerged from the shadow and advanced under the greenish gas-lamp.

'Excuse me, Sir ...'

At the sight of this slender shape and that silvery, straw-coloured hair, the stroller stopped dead. 'He's suspicious,' sighed Minne, and she dared not go on with her prepared speech.

'Whatever's this little girl doing here?'

The man's speech was slightly thick but his voice was extremely genial.

'Oh dear, it's very simple ...'

'Yes, yes. Was little girlie waiting for me?'

'You're making a mistake, Sir ...'

Minne's voice was pathetically faint. She was beginning to be frightened once more, with the fear of a child who has been found and then lost again.

'She was waiting for me,' went on the engaging voice of the cheerful drunk. 'Little girlie's cold and she's going to take me to a nice warm fire.'

'Oh! I'd like to, Sir, but ...'

The man was quite close: under the top hat she could see red cheeks and a hay-coloured beard turning grey.

'Good gracious me! Surely a child like this can't be a ... Tell me, how old are you?'

He smelt of brandy and cigar-smoke and he was breathing in short, harsh gasps. Minne, in despair, recoiled a little and flattened herself against the wall. She tried to be polite still and not to annoy him.

'I'm not quite fifteen and a half, Sir. That is what happened: I left Mamma's house ...'

'You did, eh?' he whinnied. 'Girlie shall tell me all about it in front of a nice fire, sitting on my knee.'

A fur-upholstered arm embraced Minne's waist and all her strength left her. But the breath, heavy with alcohol and cigar-smoke, on her face galvanized her out of her swoon: with a twist of her shoulders, she freed herself and became in a flash the blonde Infanta who used to terrorize Antoine.

'You don't know who you're talking to, Sir!'

He whinnied more softly.

'All right, all right! Girlie shall have anything she wants. Come on, little darling . . . Mimi . . .'

'My name isn't Mimi!'

As he was bearing down on her, Minne gave a bound and started to run again. But her lamed shoe kept slipping off at every step and she had to slow down and stop.

'He's old, he can't run after me.'

At the first turning, she held her breath and listened in terror . . . Nothing . . . Oh, yes there was! . . . A clattering of heels and a walking-stick and all at once the old man loomed up, hot in pursuit, and fell into step beside her, whinnying:

'Little darling . . . anything she wants . . . she's made me run but I've got good legs.'

The lost child dragged herself along like a partridge trailing a broken wing. There was only one thought left in her aching head: 'Perhaps, if I go on walking long enough, I'll get to the Seine and then I'll throw myself in.' She passed milk carts and slow wagons, with their drivers asleep, without seeing them. Under the rays of a street lamp she had caught sight of the old man's face and her heart had stood still. Old Corne! He was like old Corne!

'I understand! I understand now! I'm dreaming. But how long the dream is lasting and how I ache all over! If only I can wake up before the old man catches me!'

A final, supreme effort to run! She tripped on the edge of the curb and fell, bruising her knees. She got to her feet again, her dress covered with mud and one cheek splashed with it.

With a great sigh of despair, she looked all round her and

then, in the dim, grey dawn, she recognized that pavement, those bare trees, that bald slope . . . It was . . . no . . . yes! It was the Avenue Berthier . . .

'Ah!' she screamed aloud. 'It's the end of the dream! Quick, quick . . . I'll wake up when I get to the door!'

Dragging herself along she got there. The door was ajar as it was last night. She pushed against it with both hands and, as it opened, fell forward in a faint on the tiled floor of the hall.

Antoine was asleep. In the transparent sleep of the early hours of morning a thousand beauties were alternately offering themselves to him and withdrawing. All of them were called Minne and not one of them resembled the real Minne. Out of compassion for his boyish shyness and inexperience, they were as gentle as mothers and as friendly as sisters before they caressed him in a way that was neither maternal nor sisterly. And all this facile bliss was gradually being poisoned: somewhere up in the pink and blue clouds hung a clock which was going to strike seven and precipitate Antoine headlong out of his Mahomet's paradise.

Farewell, beauties! In any case, he could no longer retain them, even in his dream. Here was the dreaded sound, the seven strident bell-strokes that reverberated in the pit of his stomach. They persisted, prolonging themselves into a continuous trill that sounded so furious and so real that Antoine, well and truly awake, sat up with a start, looking as haggard as Lazarus resurrected from the tomb.

'Good Lord! Why, it's someone ringing the front-door bell!'

Antoine tumbled into his slippers and dragged on a pair of trousers.

'Papa's getting up . . . What time can it be? It's a bit thick, waking everyone up at this hour.'

He opened his door: down the passage came the sound of a tearful voice, talking hurriedly and brokenly. And suddenly Antoine felt his cheeks quiver with a peculiar tremor as he caught the sound of one name – 'Miss Minne'.

'Antoine! Bring some light, my boy!'

Antoine hunted for the candle, broke one match, then another. 'If the third doesn't strike, it means Minne's dead.'

In the waiting-room, Célénie was telling and re-telling a story which sounded like an extract from a cheap thriller:

'There she was on the ground, Sir, in a dead faint, and in such a state as you never saw! . . . Mud all over her, even in her hair, and no hat on, nothing. Of course, it's not for me to say, but it's my idea that she was abducted and they did all sorts of shocking things to her and brought her back for dead.'

'Yes . . .' said Uncle Paul, mechanically, buttoning and unbuttoning his brown pyjamas.

'Drenched to the skin, Sir, and all covered with mud!'

'Yes . . . Stop gibbering! I'll come over.'

'I'm coming with you, Papa,' said Antoine, his teeth chattering.

'No, no, my boy! There's no need whatever for you to come too. This story Célénie's been telling me is pure fantasy. Girls don't get abducted from their bedrooms!'

'I don't care what you say, Papa! I tell you I'm coming with you!' he almost screamed, on the verge of hysteria. He had understood everything! It was all true and Minne had not lied! The nights on the embankment, the inadmissible love affair, the gentleman with the dangerous career, everything, everything! And now the logical end of the tragedy had come: Minne, defiled and mortally wounded was dying over in that house.

Outside Minne's bedroom, Antoine waited, with his shoulder pressed against the wall. On the other side of that door, Uncle Paul and Mamma, bending over the mudstained bed, had just finished a terrifying examination: the lamp that Mamma was holding at arm's length tottered in her shaking hand.

'But, good Lord, she hasn't been touched! She's more intact than a baby . . . if I know anything about it!'

'You're sure, Paul? You're sure?'

'Of course I am! One doesn't need to be very astute! Do hold that lamp steady! There, there! Are you feeling faint?'

'No, no. I'm quite all right.'

Mamma smiled; a happy smile, though her lips were white. Antoine, who had been expecting a Mamma in tears, screaming and half-demented, did not know what to think when at last she opened the door to him.

'Is that you, my poor boy? Do come in ... Your father's just been ... been examining her ...'

He watched her as, with a steady hand, she held a handkerchief moistened with ether to Minne's nostrils. Minne, oh God! could that really be Minne? Lying on the bed ... the bed that was still made ... was a little beggar-girl in a pink apron all clotted with mud, a little beggar-girl with rigid feet, one of which was still wearing a heelless red slipper. All that could be seen of her face, half-hidden by the handkerchief, was the dark bar of the two closed eyelids.

'She's breathing well,' said Uncle Paul. 'Got a bit of a cold. I can't see anything the matter with her except that she's feverish. We'll know the rest later.'

A plaintive cry interrupted him. Mamma bent down over Minne with the fierce protectiveness of a mother-bitch.

'Are you there, Mamma?'

'My love?'

'Are you there ... *really* there?'

'Yes, my treasure.'

'Who's that talking? Have they gone?'

'Who? Tell me who? The people who hurt you?'

'Yes ... old Corne ... and the other one?'

Mamma lifted Minne up to a sitting position with her head on her breast. Now Antoine could recognize the pale face under the fair hair that was quite grey with dried mud. The changed colour of that dirty hair made her look as if she had suddenly grown old. Antoine burst into choking, agonizing sobs that racked his whole body.

'Hush!' said Mamma.

At the sound of the sobs, Minne's eyelids, which looked

quite blue in her waxen face, went up. The beautiful deep eyes under the noble eyebrows, distraught from what they had seen, were indeed Minne's eyes! They turned their gaze up to the ceiling, then lowered it towards Antoine who was standing there, crying without a handkerchief. A burning flush came over her pale cheeks; she seemed to be making a terrible effort as she huddled close to Mamma and stretched out her frail, mudstained hands towards Antoine.

'You know, Antoine, it wasn't true! It isn't true! None of it was true! You do believe me, don't you, that it wasn't true?'

He shook his head violently, sniffing back his tears. Utterly shattered, what he believed was that, before she had been frightened and maltreated, this charming child had willingly consented to be used as a sexual plaything, as an obscene doll, by a scoundrel – perhaps by several?

He wept for Minne and he also wept for himself because she was lost, debased, branded for ever with a hall-mark of filth.

Part Two

'I'm going to sleep with Minne!'

Little Baron Couderc announced this resolution in a firm, clear voice, then blushed violently and turned up his fur collar. With his walking-stick shouldered like a rifle, he seemed to be wishing to conquer that vast, gloomy steppe into whose smoky darkness one plunges after leaving the blinding lights of the Rue Royale. All that could be seen of him was a little of the back of a neck with fair hair cropped close on the nape and the impertinent nose of an aristocratic little hooligan. Under the trees of the Avenue Gabriel, he dared to repeat, defying the shivering back of a policeman: 'I'm going to sleep with Minne! ... It's queer,' he thought, 'apart from my little brother's English governess, the first one of all, no woman has ever made such an impression on me as this ... Minne isn't a woman like other women ...'

As he approached the Rue Christophe-Colombe, he was no longer thinking of anything but putting out the cakes and the electric kettle, and, above all, of the process of undressing Minne, which he hoped would be quick and easy and which he would have liked to skip. His extreme youth began to embarrass him. He was little Baron Couderc whom the ladies of Maxim's affectionately called 'little sledge-hammer'; he had a nose which compelled him to be impertinent, mocking short-sighted blue eyes and a fresh, full-lipped mouth; but he could not always forget that he was only twenty-two ...

'Monsieur le Baron, that lady is here,' his manservant informed him in a whisper.

'Good heavens, she's here already! What about the cakes? And the flowers – and everything else! The place will be

87

looking ghastly. Let's hope at least that there's a good fire!'

She had taken her hat off and was sitting by the fire as if she were in her own home. Her simple dress covered her feet; wisps of her fair hair, electrified by the frost, made a silvery halo round her helmet-shaped chignon. With her hands folded in her lap she looked like a typical young girl in an English illustration. Her features, almost too sharply chiselled in their delicacy, wore an expression of extreme childish seriousness. Antoine, her husband, often said to her: 'Minne, why do you look such a child when you're unhappy?'

She raised her eyes as the fair-haired young man entered and smiled at him. Her smile turned her face into a woman's. She smiled with an expression at once haughty and ready to comply with every demand which made men want to try anything, no matter what.

'Oh, Minne! How can you ever forgive me? Am I really late?'

'No. I'm early.'

They spoke almost in the same voice, he with a Parisian mannerism of pitching his high, she in an even, drawling soprano.

He sat down beside her, demoralized by their being alone together. No more friends as malicious onlookers, no more husband – an unobservant husband, it was true, but at least they could enjoy the pleasures of naughty schoolchildren in his presence: touching hands under a saucer, exchanging the gesture of a kiss behind Antoine's back. Only yesterday, little Baron Jacques could still tell himself: 'I diddle the lot: they're all completely hoodwinked.' Today, he was alone with Minne, this Minne who had arrived, completely calm, at the first rendezvous – ahead of time!

He kissed her hands, surreptitiously observing her. She bent her head and smiled her arrogant, equivocal smile. Then he flung himself greedily on Minne's mouth and, half-kneeling, fastened his lips long and thirstily on it, without a word, suddenly so ardent that one of his knees trembled uncontrollably in an involuntary St Vitus's dance.

With her head thrown back, she was choking a little. Her pile of fair hair was pulling away from the pins and on the point of tumbling down in a smooth cascade.

'Wait!' she whispered.

He unlocked his arms and stood up. The lamp lit his face up from below; a changed face with blanched nostrils, vivid bitten lips and a trembling chin, all its still childish features suddenly aged by desire which at once ravaged and ennobled them.

Minne remained seated, staring up at him with a docile, anxious expression. While she was securing her chignon, her lover seized her wrists.

'Oh Minne, don't put your hair up again!'

It was the first time he had used the intimate 'tu' in addressing her. She flushed a little, half offended, half pleased and lowered her lashes that were darker than her hair.

'Perhaps I love him?' she wondered secretly.

He knelt down, stretching out his hands towards Minne's blouse with its evidently complicated hooks and eyes and the double buttonholes of its starched collar. She saw Jacques' half-open mouth on the level of her lips, a child's panting mouth parched with the thirst to kiss her. Putting her arms round his neck, she spontaneously kissed that mouth like an over-fond sister or an innocently bold fiancée. He groaned and pushed her away with feverish, clumsy hands.

'Wait!' she reiterated.

Standing up, she calmly began to undo her white collar and her silk blouse, then her pleated skirt which dropped off at once to the floor. Half turning towards Jacques, she said, with a smile:

'You've no idea how heavy these pleated skirts are!'

He rushed forward to pick it up.

'No, leave it. I take my petticoat and skirt off together, one inside the other. It's easier to put them on again, you see.'

He nodded to show that he did, indeed, see. He saw Minne, in her drawers, calmly continuing to undress. Not enough hips or bosom to give her any resemblance to the curvaceous female popularly considered desirable. She still looked a young girl, because of the simplicity of her gestures and her elegant angularity and also because of the long, tight-fitting drawers which disdained fashion and came below the knee, emphasizing its delicate, clear-cut outline.

'Marvellous legs! Like a page's!' he exclaimed aloud. The pounding of his heart made his tonsils feel swollen and painful.

Minne made a little grimace, then smiled. She seemed to be overcome by a sudden modesty when she had to undo her four suspenders but, once she was in her chemise, she recovered her calm and methodically arranged her two rings and the ruby stud which fastened her collar to her blouse on the velvet-draped mantelpiece.

She saw herself in the glass; pale, young and naked under the fine chemise. As her silvery-gold helmet of hair was toppling over one ear she undid it and laid her tortoise-shell hair-pins out in a row. One puff of hair remained pulled down over her forehead and she said:

'When I was little, Mamma used to do my hair like that.'

Overcome by seeing Minne almost naked, Jacques hardly heard her. He was overwhelmed by a huge, bitter wave of love, of genuine love, furious and jealous and vindictive.

'Minne!'

Struck by the new note in his voice, she came nearer to him, veiled in her fair hair, holding her hands like shells over her tiny breasts.

'Whatever's the matter?'

She was close against him now, warm from the heavy dress she had taken off. Her sharp scent of lemon verbena made him think of summer, of thirst, of cool shade.

'Oh, Minne!' he sobbed. 'Swear to me you've never done this for anyone else.'

'For anyone else?'

'For anyone else, in front of anyone else. Never arranged your rings and your hairpins like that, never said that your mother used to do your hair like that ... that you've never, in fact, that you've never ...'

He was gripping her so hard in his arms that she bent backwards like a too tightly bound sheaf of corn and her hair brushed the carpet.

'Swear to you that I've never . . . Oh, how silly you are!'

He kept her tight against him, enchanted by her telling him he was being silly. He contemplated her from close to, as she lay bent back almost double over his arm, curiously observing the texture of her skin, the veins on her temple, green as rivers, the dark eyes in which the light danced. He remembered having gloated with the same passion over the pearly blue scales, the feathery antennae, all the marvels of a beautiful live butterfly he had caught one day in the holidays. But Minne allowed herself to be scrutinized without beating her wings.

A clock struck and they both started.

'Five o'clock,' sighed Minne. 'We must hurry up.'

Jacques' two arms slid down, stroking Minne's slender hips. The conceited egotism of his age nearly completely betrayed itself in a boast:

'Oh, *I've* . . .'

He was going to say, like a bragging young cock: '*I've* still plenty of time – it never takes *me* long!' But he checked himself, shamed before this child who had taught him so many things all at once. In a few minutes he had become aware of jealousy, of self-mistrust, of a little spasm of the heart he had never known before, and of that delicate fatherliness a man of twenty can suddenly feel for a frail, naked creature who trusts him and who might perhaps cry out with pain in the act of love.

Minne did not cry out. All Jacques saw under his lips was the strange, pure face of a visionary and wide-open dark eyes that stared far into the distance, beyond modesty, beyond himself, with the ardent, disappointed expression of Sister Ann on the watch-tower. Minne, crushed down on the bed, endured her lover like an eager martyr, exalting in his tortures, and tried to induce the climax of passion by rhythmically writhing her body. But she did not cry out, either with pain or pleasure, and when he collapsed on top of her, with his eyes closed, his nostrils pale and pinched and his breath coming in sobs, she merely twisted her head, so that her silvery hair fell in a flood outside the bed, to have a better look at him.

They had to part while Jacques was still caressing her with the frenzy of a lover about to die and endlessly kissing that slender body which she made no attempt to defend. Now he would carefully trace its contours with his forefinger as if he were drawing it, now he would grip Minne's knees between his own so hard that he hurt her or, cruel in his infatuation, try to crush the faint rise of her breasts flat under his palms ... He bit her on the shoulder while she was dressing again; she snarled and turned on him like a wild beast ... then suddenly she laughed and exclaimed:

'Oh, those eyes! How funny your eyes look!'

In the glass he saw that his face did indeed look funny: dark rings round his eyes, his mouth red and swollen, his hair in wisps over his eyebrows. It looked at once sad and debauched, but there was something else too in its expression, something ardent, yet utterly exhausted, which could not be put into words.

'Nasty little thing! Let me see yours.'

He seized her by the wrists but she freed herself and pointed a menacing finger at him.

'If you don't let me get away, I won't come back again! Ugh! How awful it's going to be outside after this nice warm bed and this fire and this pink lamp.'

'And me, Minne! Will you do me the favour of regretting me, next after the pink lamp?'

'That depends,' she said, as she put on her toque trimmed with white camellias. 'Yes, if you get me a cab at once.'

'The rank's quite close,' sighed Jacques, brushing his hair in a hit-or-miss fashion. 'Bother! There's no more hot water!'

'There very seldom *is* enough hot water,' murmured Minne absentmindedly.

He stared at her with raised eyebrows. In putting on his clothes he had gradually put on the face of 'little Baron Couderc' again.

'My dear girl you sometimes say things, things ... that could make me doubt you, or else doubt my own ears!'

Minne did not consider it necessary to reply. She was standing in the doorway, slim and modest in her dark clothes, her eyes far away ... already gone.

'One more!' thought Minne crudely.

She leant an angry shoulder against the faded upholstery of the cab and threw back her head, not from fear of being seen but from horror of everything that was going on outside.

'Well, that's over ... One more! The third, and with no success. It's enough to make one give up. If my first lover, the house surgeon at the hospital, hadn't assured me that I'm "perfectly formed for love" I'd go and consult a great specialist.'

She went over all the details of her brief rendezvous and clenched her fists inside her muff.

'After all, that boy is as nice as anything! He was dying of pleasure in my arms and there was I waiting and saying to myself: "Obviously, it's not unpleasant ... but show me something better!"'

'It's like it was with my second, that Italian Antoine met at Pleyel's ... what was his name? ... the one who had teeth right up to his eyes ... Diligenti! When I asked him for what they call in books "infamous practices", he laughed and then he started all over again doing exactly what he'd just been doing! That's my luck, that's my life and I'm getting fed up with it.'

She did not think of Antoine at that moment except vaguely to shift the responsibility on to him. 'I bet it's his fault that I feel about as much pleasure as ... as this seat. He must have wrenched something delicate inside me.'

'Poor Minne!' she sighed. The cab was nearing the Place de L'Étoile. In a few minutes she would be at home, in the Avenue de Villiers, just by the Place Péreire. She would cross the icy pavement, climb the overheated staircase that smelt of fresh cement and putty – and then there would be

Antoine's great arms and his joyous dog-like welcome. She lowered her head in resignation. There was no more hope for today.

Two years of marriage, and three lovers ... Lovers? Could she really call them that in her memory? She could only think of them with faintly vindictive indifference, those men who had experienced in her arms the brief, convulsive bliss that she sought with a persistence that was already becoming discouraged. She forgot them, relegated them to a dim corner of her mind where she could no longer recollect their features, hardly even their names. Only one memory remained, vivid and clear-cut, the memory of her wedding night.

Minne could still have drawn with her finger the shadow on her bedroom wall that caricatured Antoine that night: a back hunched with effort, wisps of hair standing up like horns, a short satyr's beard – the whole fantastic image of Pan labouring to seduce a nymph.

Antoine had responded to her sharp cry when he wounded her by an idiotic demonstration of joyous gratitude, tender fussing and brotherly fondling ... it was high time!

She had ground her teeth and not cried. She had breathed in the smell of a naked man with no more than surprise. Nothing had intoxicated her, not even her pain – burning oneself with hot curling tongs could hurt more – but she had wished that she could die, without much hope that she would. When her brand-new husband, her ardent, clumsy husband had fallen asleep, she had timidly tried to escape from the arms that were still closed round her. But her soft, silky hair, enmeshed in Antoine's fingers, held her captive. All the rest of the night, Minne had lain with her head pulled back, patient and unmoving, thinking of what had just happened to her, of ways of arranging things, of the profound mistake of having married this species of brother.

'It's Mamma's fault, when you really think it over. Poor Mamma! She remained convinced that it was written on my

94

forehead: "This is the girl who stayed out all night!" Stayed out all night! A lot I got out of that! It was no good my telling her that all I did was to meet two women and an old man and catch a bad cold. Uncle Paul cold-shoulders me now that Mamma's dead, as if I were the cause of her death. Poor Mamma, she couldn't find anything better to say to me before she left us than: "Marry Antoine, darling: he loves you and you can never marry anyone else." Nonsense! I could have married thirty-six thousand others, and it wouldn't have mattered which other, provided it wasn't this one!'

Since her marriage, Minne had remained imprisoned in her past without suspecting that it is not normal for a woman, still hardly more than a child, to begin her meditations with 'In the old days . . .'

As to the dream which had once impelled her towards the future, towards Curly and the mysterious world that came to life at night in the shadow of the fortifications, she seemed to have awakened from it, frightened, with no clear recollection of it. But, disappointed, humiliated and better informed, she was beginning to guess that the great Adventure was Love and that there was no other. But what sort of love? 'Oh!' Minne implored inwardly, 'Oh, for a love, no matter what kind, a love like everyone else's, but a real one. I know for certain that, with that real one, I could create a love that would be worthy of me alone!'

'Oh, I was sure that ring was my Minne! I bet you're going to be cross with me because you're late!'

She smiled, although she did not feel in the least like laughing, at knowing how much her unjustified bad temper had been foreseen and allowed for. Deep down, she was not displeased to see him again, this tall boy with the equine face – handsome, if you like – whose youthfulness he now adorned with a serious beard. 'At least,' she thought, as she unfastened her veil, 'I'm sure of this one. I don't expect anything more of him. That's something, at the point I've reached now.'

'Why "late"? We're dining at home, I presume?'

Antoine threw up scandalized arms which nearly touched the ceiling.

'Good Lord! What about the Chaulieus?'

'Oh dear!' said Minne.

And she remained rooted to the spot in consternation, her veil stretched taut between her delicate fingers. She looked so enchanting, with that face like a scolded child's, that Antoine flung himself on her, lifted her off the ground and tried to kiss her. But she hastily disengaged herself, her eyes cold again.

'There you go, making me later still! Anyway they dine so late there. We shall never be the last to arrive!'

She glided towards the door of her bedroom, then turned round again, her lips puckered in a pout.

'Do you really want to go to this dinner?'

Antoine opened his mouth, then shut it, then opened it again, evidently about to produce such a flood of urgent reasons that Minne lost her temper and burst out, before he had spoken:

'Yes, *I* know! Your relations with Pleyel! And the publicity in the papers Chaulieu finances! And Lugné-Poë who wants to order a *barbytos* for Isadora Duncan's dances! I know the whole lot, I tell you! I'll be ready in ten minutes!'

'Since she knows all that,' thought Antoine, left standing all alone in the middle of the drawing-room, 'why does she ask me if I really want to go to this dinner?'

Antoine's love was as incapable of deceit as it was of moderation. His tenderness made him too tender, his gaiety too gay and his anxiety too anxious. Perhaps there were no other barriers between her and himself, than this need – 'this mania', Minne said – for being sincere and straightforward? One day, Uncle Paul, Antoine's father, had said to his son, in front of Minne: 'One must mistrust one's first impulses!' 'Oh, that's certainly true,' Minne had meekly answered, adding mentally: 'Most of all, people who don't lie spontaneously. They're lazy creatures who won't even take the trouble to arrange the truth a little, even if only out of politeness or to be intriguing.'

Antoine was one of these incorrigibles. Every minute he kept exclaiming to Minne: 'I love you!' And it was true. It was true in an absolute way, without the slightest variation, now and forever.

'Where should we be,' philosophized Minne, 'if I stated *my* feelings as positively as he does? Suppose I exclaimed with the same conviction as his: "I don't love you!" '

Once again, as so often, left deserted in the white drawing-room, he was having a straightforward argument with the absent Minne: 'Why did she ask me, since she already knew?' he puzzled, as he paced to and fro. In passing, he bumped against the *barbytos* he had had built at Pleyel's. The great lyre emitted a sad, harmonious moan. 'Good heavens! My Model Eight!' He fingered its strings solicitously and, catching sight of himself in the glass, smiled at the image it presented of a bearded rhapsodist.

Antoine was not a genius, but he had the good sense to realize it. Tormented by the desire to make himself more impressive in Minne's eyes, he had obtained permission from his chief, Gustave Lyon, to devote some hours of the time he was officially supposed to spend on the Pleyel Company's accounts, to reconstructing Greek and Egyptian musical instruments. 'I might be equally well employed on motor-cars,' he admitted to himself, 'but the reconstruction of the *barbytos* might perhaps earn me a scrap of red ribbon in my buttonhole.'

The door of the bedroom opened again; Antoine started.

'I said ten minutes,' exclaimed a triumphant little voice. 'Look at your watch!'

'It's marvellous,' admitted this model husband. 'How beautiful you are, Minne!'

Beautiful, one could not be quite sure; but unusual and charming, as she always had been. She was wearing a greenish-blue or bluish-green tulle dress, the colour of an aquamarine. A silver belt, a silver rose at the edge of the discreet décolletage, that was all. But there were Minne's fragile shoulders, Minne's glittering hair, the astonishing black eyes that did not go with the rest, and, below her necklace – the pearls were no bigger than rice grains – two tiny salt-cellars that were oddly touching.

'Come along, my pet!'

When the Chaulieus give a dinner-party everyone arrives in a combative mood, fists clenched and chin set defensively. Really strong characters affect an air of ease and well-being, the relaxed face of a good friend come to spend a quiet evening with good friends. But these are rare. As a general rule, when a man announces during the day: 'I'm dining with the Chaulieus tonight,' faces turn towards him with sarcastic interest. People say 'Aha!' and this means: 'Best of luck! Are you feeling in good form? Biceps up to scratch?'

Shorn of all legend, there was nothing about the Chaulieus to alarm the bolder spirits; Madame Chaulieu was a harpy, granted. But there still existed peaceable souls on whom this revelation produced no more effect that if they had been told, for example: 'Madame Chaulieu is slightly hunchbacked.'

This remarkable woman paraded her malice as others parade their vices. Being a practical person, she had first of all made herself known by talking of herself, herself and nothing but herself. Patiently, for five or six years, she had begun all her sentences with: 'I, who am the most malicious woman in Paris ...' And, nowadays, Paris repeated with touching unanimity: 'Madame Chaulieu, who is the most malicious woman in Paris ...'

Perhaps, with her, it was no more than unemployed surplus energy, the energy of a hunchback whose hump is within; for her small body carried the large and magnificent head of an oriental Jewess with stately erectness.

Chaulieu, her husband, who looked like a little snub-nosed hidalgo, was a modest, discouraged, hard-working man, terrified of his partner. People were apt to refer to him as 'Poor Chaulieu' when they spoke of him for he allowed the melancholy of an incurable but resigned invalid to appear on his face. He proudly accepted the misfortune of being his wife's husband and his silence signified: 'Leave me in peace. I don't need your pity. If I'm her husband, it's because I wanted to be!'

Irène Chaulieu dressed expensively. She wore white lace or tulle dresses that would have benefited considerably from more frequent visits to the cleaners', second-hand sables and white gloves, always slightly split on account of the nervous fidgetiness of her small hands. They were damp hands, always pawing something, so that they collected dust from knick-knacks, sugar from cakes, butter from sandwiches and black smears from a silver chain round her neck that they were perpetually fiddling.

When Irène Chaulieu gave a dinner-party, she received her guests sitting on the extreme edge of a chair to make herself look taller, at the far end of an immense drawing-room, facing the door so that she could stare at her friends the moment they entered and keep her fine eyes fixed on them with a ruthless, malevolent gaze as they crossed the parquet floor that glittered like a lake.

Such was the strange woman friend that chance had provided for Minne. Irène had pounced on this young woman with the collector's curiosity which made her so affable to newcomers and enlivened her with the joy of getting to know someone, picking them to pieces and destroying them. And, besides, Antoine was not so bad – tall and bearded and looking like a respectable Brazilian. Irène's far-sighted sensuality always had an eye to the future.

'Oh, here they are at last!'

Minne glided across the slippery parquet like a skater, followed by Antoine, who muttered apologies and prostrated himself over Madame Chaulieu's outstretched hand. But she did not even look at him; she was busy taking in every detail of what Minne was wearing.

'Was it that lovely dress, dear, that made you so late?'

It was a sarcastic rebuke, rather than a question, but Minne did not seem annoyed. She was counting the male guests with dark, serious eyes and forgot to say How-do-you-do to Chaulieu, who exclaimed in a voice that sounded weary, even in its excitement:

'Minne, our friend Maschaing wants to meet you.'

This time Minne seemed to be aroused from her indifference. Maschaing, the Academician – *the* Maschaing who had written *Spectre d'Orient* and *Les Désabusées*, Maschaing in person! 'There's a man who ought to know all about erotic pleasures!' Minne told herself. She bowed very graciously to a little man who was bowing to her. 'Hmm, I'd have thought he'd be younger! And besides, he's not looking at me hard enough. It's a pity!'

Irène Chaulieu stood up, trailing two yards of dusty guipure lace and took possession of Maschaing's arm. Her regal, hook-nosed head and her small body, stiffly upright on perilously high heels proclaimed the pride of the successful lion-hunter: 'I've got him at last, this academician of theirs!'

'Maugis,' she threw over her shoulder, 'you're taking Minne in to dinner.'

Minne followed, her gloved hand on the sleeve of Maugis, whom she had never seen before at such close quarters. 'He's a funny man, my neighbour. He's got snail's eyes. But I rather like that military moustache. And, besides, his nose is too short, which amuses me. He's supposed to lead what's called a gay life, isn't he? Irène says you can learn a lot from these men of the older generation. In fact, if he shaved off his side-whiskers, he'd lose the most characteristic part of his face. I've got a pain in my back, why? Goodness, I'd nearly forgotten! Of course, it was that little Couderc today.' She smiled coldly at the memory, and refused the soup.

On her left, Chaulieu was prudently drinking Vichy water with an air of resignation for, as he said: 'There's no house where the food is worse than in mine.' On her right, Maugis was watching her with his protruding eyes. Opposite her, Irène Chaulieu, very tall now that she was sitting down, was gulping down her soup, dipping one end of a scarf into it, adding new stains to several previous ones, and 'softening up' Maschaing. She was working on him with that cruelty in her praise and that cynicism in her admiration which sometimes subjugated their object and brought him, passive and happy to Irène's greedy, well-chiselled lips and into her muscular, female lion-tamer's arms.

Antoine smiled at his wife. She returned his smile, throwing back her head so that Maugis should follow the line of her neck and notice the brilliance of her eyes between her fair lashes. 'You never know,' she thought.

At the two far ends of the table were various dim people, poor relations of Irène's, young literary prodigies who had not yet taken their degree but who regarded Mallarmé as a reactionary; an American, known as 'the beautiful Suzie' without any further designation and her boy-friend of the week; a Hebrew jewel merchant whom the hostess, who coveted a star-sapphire would shortly be vainly cajoling with her most explicit looks and her sisterly cynicism: 'We two, who are thorough scoundrels . . .' A fair-haired pianist who played Beethoven was announced to be arriving at eleven.

Minne gazed round at all these people and laughed. 'Poor Antoine, he's landed with Aunt Rachel again! It's what always happens. As he's the only man here with good manners, they shove all the old female relatives on to him.'

'You're not drinking, Madame?'

'Aha! So that fat Maugis has made up his mind has he? All the same, that moustache! I can't get used to hearing that piping voice of his coming out of that shaggy bush. He sounds like a girl with a slight cold.'

'Oh yes, I am! I'm drinking champagne and water.'

'And how right you are! Champagne is the only tolerable wine in this house. Chaulieu does the advertising for Pommery, luckily for you!'

'I didn't know. Suppose Irène heard you!'

'No danger! She's wearing herself out arranging corsage effects for Maschaing's benefit.'

'That's where you're wrong, my dear Maugis. I always hear everything.'

Irène shot a deadly look at the foolhardy wretch who promptly bowed his back and stretched out his clasped hands.

'Beg pardon! Won't do it again,' he whined.

But Irène Chaulieu was not so easily disarmed.

'Don't get in my bad books, my dear Maugis: it might cost you dear.'

Piqued at being threatened in front of Minne, the man with the huge moustache became insolent.

'Your threat doesn't perturb me in the least, dear lady. Women have never cost me anything and I'm hanged if I'm going to change my habits for you!'

Irène Chaulieu was snuffing the wind like a war-horse and about to reply. Already the guests had fallen silent and were leaning forward as if they were at the theatre. The tired gentle voice of Chaulieu – what a pity! – averted the storm.

'I *told* you the timbale would be a failure!'

Although the assertion was strictly true, the guests cast

ferocious glances at this martyr. Chaulieu had made them miss one of those scathing reprimands which were the speciality of the house and besides, as Maugis said, during that time, people would not have noticed what they were eating. Nevertheless Minne bestowed a singularly flattering glance on her brave neighbour. 'His moustache doesn't lie: he's a hero!' The hero himself felt the inferior kind of sympathy, the weakness of the little society woman for the wrestler who has just 'thrown' an adversary emanating from her to him. He was ready to take advantage of it, attracted by Minne's disturbing beauty, her charm of a curio not for sale.

The dinner-party was thawing. Irène Chaulieu was in blazing form, intoxicated by her first skirmish. She had stopped eating and was talking deliriously, pouring new calumnies into the attentive ear of the academician who was taking mental notes. Antoine was horrified to hear her defending a newly-made friend as follows:

'No, *cher maître*, you mustn't repeat such infamous gossip! Madame Barnery is a respectable woman who has never had the relations with Claudie people say. Madame Barnery has lovers.'

'What – male lovers?'

'Of course! And it's her right to have lovers! It's the right of every woman whom life has cheated! And I'll never allow anyone to speak of her in front of me in ambiguous terms!'

Antoine was staggered.

'Heaven help us if that harpy ever takes a dislike to Minne!' he groaned inwardly. 'My pure little Minne! How she's laughing at that fat journalist's jokes! Nothing of that sort even enters her mind.'

Minne was indeed laughing, with her head thrown back so that one could see the laugh rippling in waves under the pearly skin of her neck right down to the two touching little salt-cellars. She was laughing to make herself look more attractive and to avoid having to reply to the excited Maugis who was vehemently describing his state of mind to her:

'... and you would see such a fabulous love-nest, with such divans!'

'Divans!' repeated Minne, suddenly very demure. 'Monsieur Chaulieu, do you hear what my next-door neighbour is saying?'

'Certainly I hear,' replied Chaulieu, 'but I was discreetly pretending to be the gentleman enjoying his salad. And goodness, how nasty it is! Whatever is the olive oil made of in this house?'

Minne plucked his sleeve roguishly.

'Do protect me, Monsieur Chaulieu! He's saying horrible things to me!'

Chaulieu turned his snub-nosed face towards her.

'What? My poor child, are you already having to appeal for help? In that case, hadn't you better ask . . .'

'Ask who?' said Minnie very coquettishly.

Chaulieu jerked his chin towards Antoine.

'Why . . . that man over there, who looks as if his biceps were something to reckon with. Eh, Maugis, what would you say?'

Maugis, secretly annoyed, grinned and leaned his elbows heavily on the table, exaggerating the strength of his broad back.

'As long as the wife has weaknesses, I don't care a damn how strong the husband is!'

'So you say!'

'In any case, little blonde lady, your husband seems thoroughly occupied at the moment, doesn't he?'

He certainly *was* thoroughly occupied. As soon as Irène Chaulieu had seen what Maugis was up to, she had turned her back on the Immortal and flung herself on Minne's husband, the enemy. She hid the whole of one side of the table from him with her mass of puffed-up, insecurely pinned hair, her open fan and one shoulder that had escaped from its strap. She was stupefying him with words and revealing a new-found and passionate interest in the *barbytos*.

'But, my dear man, it's a revolution in music!'

'Oh, that's saying too much,' said the honest Antoine.

'Nonsense, you're too modest. Oh, if only I were a man!

Between us, we could shake the world! When one has your strength, your youth, your . . .'

Irène's beautiful oriental eyes gazed deep into Antoine's; her heavily mascaraed lashes fluttered lazily, like the wings of a settled butterfly. He blinked, embarrassed, and tired, too, by the harsh electric light which fell on the embroidered tablecloth and was reflected upwards in a pallid glare on people's faces. The distant sound of a door-bell put an end to his torture. Chaulieu drew his wife's attention to it with a little click of the tongue:

'Hup! Irène.'

She rose reluctantly, wrapping her scarf round her, sweeping up some banana skins that had got entangled in it as she did so and said at the top of her voice:

'People already turning up after dinner! Before they've even finished picking their teeth. I shall find plenty more heads at an angle of forty-five degrees in the drawing-room. Well, *I* can't help it if everyone wants to dine here. Minne, you must be the daughter of the house with the coffee and liqueurs.'

Minne did not dislike this delicate office which consisted in manipulating fragile cups, a coffee-pot and a pair of sugar-tongs in an overcrowded drawing-room. She performed it with careful hands and gave a convincing imitation of a demure young girl waiting on her mother's guests which made the men, replete with food and drink, feel sentimental.

'What a pleasure a little wife like that would be, old man. Doesn't that charming little mug make you think how nice it would be to see her darning one's socks?'

Maugis' enthusiasm was now beyond all bounds. He had just confided to a young poet, too young not to be blasé about the beauty of women:

'What a little neck to strangle! And that hair! And those eyes! And those . . .'

Irène Chaulieu, whose figure had suddenly appeared beside him, interrupted mockingly:

'There, there, Maugis, calm down! You must at least

admit I'm a good friend. I kept the husband busy at dinner to leave the coast clear for you.'

'That's true, I'll give you credit for that. She's awfully charming, that child! I bet my bottom dollar that if I met her on a desert island . . .'

'My poor Maugis, I'm sorry for you. There's nothing doing with Minne.'

The writer shrugged his heavy shoulders.

'She's virtuous? All the better! A woman who hasn't slept around is less suspicious.'

'That depends,' Irène said coolly, lowering her eyelashes. 'There are women to whom men mean nothing.'

In order to listen better, Maugis threw his cigarette into a vase of roses.

'No? Really? Her? Tell me all! We two are good old pals, aren't we, Irène?'

'Yes, at the moment,' she scoffed. 'But you're too much of a scandalmonger, my fat friend, you shan't know a thing.'

Assured of having sown the good seed of a lie, she went off calmly to meet some arriving couples. Couples were rare at the Chaulieus' parties. Bachelors were there in abundance, also married men who had come without their wives. She smiled at the new arrivals and held out her hands with their highly-polished nails. The great icy drawing-room was at last filling with people and no longer echoed like a room in a house to let. Irène allowed cigars and Minne, looking so virtuous and demure in her blue dress, was busy pouring out the liqueurs.

'A little dry curaçao, Monsieur?'

There was no reply. Minne raised her eyes and found herself face to face with little Baron Couderc who had just come in. He could not get over it. Why had she not told him that he would see her tonight? And why did she not show any sign of emotion? After all, it was barely five hours since, over there in the Rue Christophe-Colombe, she had been undoing her suspenders with such charming and amusingly misplaced modesty. At the memory of that, he choked a little and his fresh, childish complexion suddenly flushed crimson.

'Why, so you're here?' he muttered.

'It seems so,' she mocked, smiling at him with her eyes.

She left a full glass in his fingers and went off, an indifferent Hebe, to offer one to Antoine.

Irène Chaulieu had seen . . . So had Maugis.

'Good Lord, Irène, what's come over the boy?' he whispered, violently interested. 'Did you see how he winced?'

'Are you surprised? I'm not. Why, didn't you know? That little Couderc is mad about her, but she couldn't care less. She must have snubbed him again, and pretty severely. He'd do well to keep out of her way in future!'

'He can't get over it; look at him. Poor kid, I feel sorry for him.'

'Sorry! My dear man, you're incredible, expecting all women to spend their time in bachelors' flats! It served little Couderc right! Personally, I like women who behave themselves.'

All the same, it was true that Jacques Couderc was suffering. He was new to this state of being in love and it made him almost unbearably impatient and uneasy. The week before, his flirtation with Minne had given him a delicious thrill, the excitement produced by a light wine that goes to one's head but does not deprive one of the use of one's legs. He would have liked to fight in her presence, insult the whole world, carry off another woman so that Minne should know about it and admire him; but he had not been tormented by this morose and ardent love, so close to tears and violence, which had emerged in that first hour of possession from the dark lair where it lay sleeping, fully armed.

Jacques was suffering from jealousy, because he was in love, and his affliction gave him a slightly awkward, hunched look as if he were prematurely rheumatic.

Ignoring the pianist who was giving a tumultuous rendering of Liszt, Maugis had rejoined Minne and Couderc was watching her cooing and laughing.

'She only laughed once today,' he thought. 'That was when she told me I was silly. Lord! I'm a lot sillier than

107

she thinks. What a revolting face he has, that Maugis! He looks like the "Frog Prince" in Walter Crane's illustrations. I don't care, I'm going to put a flea in her husband's ear!'

Jacques Couderc stuck his street-urchin's nose up in the air again, fixed on his sidelong smile and went off boldly to 'tell tales' to Antoine, who was peacefully smoking by the poker-table among the group of middle-aged men. His beard and his serious equine face had made him many acquaintances among men older than himself. And, besides, the renovator of the *barbytos* could not fool about with frivolous young idlers!

Antoine gave Jacques a fatherly smile as they shook hands.

'Have you seen my wife?'

'Yes ... that's to say, she was talking to Monsieur Maugis so I thought I ought not to ...'

'You don't know Maugis?'

'Only by sight. Is he a personal friend of yours?'

'No, certainly not. I just meet him here and at other places. He amuses Minne.'

Jacques gave Antoine a furious glance.

'Charming fellow, of course. A bit of a gay dog, but when one's a bachelor, well, you know how it is?'

'You should know better than anyone!'

'Oh, I wouldn't say that!' Jacques exclaimed with a sudden blush of unwonted modesty. 'I know people have a mania for saying I lead a terrifically gay life, but honestly that's frightfully exaggerated. At any rate *I* haven't got the unfortunate reputation Maugis has of sleeping with old ladies!'

Antoine raised his eyebrows and glanced across at Maugis who was still sitting beside Minne.

'What? He sleeps with old ladies?'

'Old ladies is saying a bit too much. With one old lady, a peroxide blonde of goodness knows what age. And heaven knows why, because he normally prefers very young girls.'

'Really? It's amazing!' declared Antoine.

His tone revealed such lively admiration that little Couderc became indignant.

'I think it's absolutely disgusting. Surely you do too?'

'Me? Why, my dear chap, I think it's marvellous! You could put me in a bed with an old woman for seven years and I'd remain like – like an . . . I can't say what!'

Baron Couderc rose to his feet, disappointed.

'You'll excuse me, won't you? I think Madame Minne is beckoning to me.'

Minne was not beckoning, she was frowning hard at him. She had been watching him and she sensed the beginning of a danger which needed to be met with boldness and cunning. She stared defiantly at Jacques as he came towards her. All the same, he was nice, that boy, and so well dressed!

'Maugis' trousers are like corkscrews and, what's more, I don't like those moiré revers. But, definitely, Jacques is too young. The way he started and turned scarlet when he found me here! I ought never to have counted on a boy as young as that to make me a woman like other women. When I think what Marthe Payet said the other day: "I'm like Bilitis: when I'm with my lover, the ceiling could fall and I wouldn't even notice it!" Jacques is like Bilitis too. Oh, I could hit him!'

She turned a little towards Maugis, whose breath she could feel on her shoulder: 'One can't reproach *him* with being too young – on the contrary! He's not handsome. But his assurance, his girlish voice, his sarcastic flattery and that – something or other . . .' She broke off, trying to think what it was and concluded, resignedly, 'Ah, of course! That something or other about any man one hardly knows!'

Jacques was now beside her and she extended her un-gloved hand to him. He brushed it with his lips and waited for an introduction to Maugis which was not forth-coming. Maugis went on smoking and staring up vaguely at the mottled blue ceiling. At last Minne got up, smoothed out her dress and walked over to the table where the refresh-ments were set out, so that her lover could follow her.

'Would you be kind enough to give me a glass of orange-ade?' he said aloud, then, very low: 'Minne, you knew that you were coming here tonight and you didn't tell me.'

'Quite true,' she admitted. 'I just didn't think about it.'

She was standing sideways to him as she spoke, holding a glass between her fingers. The harsh light beat down on her profile; her upswept lashes were like arrows launched by her watchful eyes and the small quantity of champagne she had drunk tinged the complicated whorls of her little ears with pink.

'Minne,' he went on, enraged by her very charm, 'swear that you didn't want to keep me in the dark about your flirtation with that revolting man!'

She started but did not turn towards Jacques.

'I'm not aware of knowing any revolting man. And how dare you speak to me like that – today of *all* days?'

He flung his half-eaten sandwich across the table where it landed in the brandied cherries.

'It's only since today that I *can* speak to you like that – because it's only since today I've known what suffering was – only since today that I love you!'

Minne turned round sharply: she probed deep into her lover's defiant, unhappy eyes with her serious gaze.

'Since today? Because you've had me? You really mean it? Oh, do explain to me how love can come out of a thing like that? Tell me, you love me more because of this afternoon?'

He thought he understood, but he was wrong. He thought that Minne wanted to rekindle his imagination at the fire of a very recent memory, that she wanted to enjoy, in front of everyone, the exquisite, outrageous pleasure of making him evoke every detail. His sanguine boyish complexion alternately flushed and paled; once again, he was changed and defenceless, as she had seen him just now in the Rue Christophe-Colombe.

'Oh, Minne, when you bent down to undo your suspenders . . .'

He trembled all over as he raved; his left knee twitched as it had done over there. Minne listened to him, very serious, without lowering her eyes or flinching at the burning words and when he stopped, ashamed and intoxicated, she made only one almost inaudible exclamation – of discouragement:

'It's inconceivable!'

For a Parisienne who often went out at night, Minne got up early. By nine o'clock she had had her bath and was thoroughly awake and eating her hot rolls with zest in her white dressing-room. On every floor of the brand-new house there was the same white dressing-room, the same little pearl-grey drawing-room, the same big drawing-room with bay windows. It was deplorably unimaginative but Minne never thought about it.

This morning, wrapped in her white bath-robe that looked like a monk's habit, her long golden plait flapping against her back, she was savouring to the full the exquisite solitude that followed her husband's daily departure to work.

Until midday, she would be alone, free to do as she liked: smooth her shining hair back quite flat which made her face look Japanese, study the weather, run a pointed finger-nail into small corners to verify that they had been properly dusted, trim a hat with a bird of paradise feather that fluttered in her breath like a meadow-grass, free to dream, to read, to write, to enjoy the intoxicating solitude on which Minne had always depended for counsel. It was on a bright, crisp winter morning like this that she had gone round to see Diligenti, an Italian who was some sort of composer. She had found him at his piano, half-flattered, half-annoyed and not knowing what to do. To punish her for disturbing him at that hour, he had made passionate love to her, but had left her disappointed. But today Minne felt like a sensible house-wife. Yesterday's disappointment – her fourth – had made her think seriously and she was thinking very seriously indeed over her empty cup.

'I must do something about it. Definitely, I must do something about it. I don't yet know what. But things can't go on like this. I can't go around from bed to bed giving pleasure to Mr So-and-So and Mr What's-His-Name for the sole satisfaction of feeling slightly bruised all over and having to do my hair again, not to mention that my shoes are all cold when I put them on again and sometimes wet as well. Whatever must I look like? Irène Chaulieu says you must spare yourself if you don't want straight away to look fifty. She assures me that as long as you cry out "Ah! Ah!" and clench your fists and pretend to choke, that completely satisfies *them*. Perhaps that satisfies men, but it doesn't satisfy me!'

The arrival of an express letter interrupted Minne's bitter reflections.

'It's from Jacques. Already!'

Minne darling, Minne of my dreams, Minne whom I love so terribly, I'm expecting you here today. I can't tell you, my dear little queen, all that you have brought into my life, but, since yesterday, I know for an absolute certainty that if I can't see you as often as I want to the whole world will collapse! Don't laugh, Minne. I'm not boasting when I tell you I should never have suspected that such a thing could happen to me. Are you love? Are you a disease of my brain? You most certainly are not happiness, Minne darling,
                                                                    Jacques

She tore the note into tiny scraps with vindictive roughness.

'And is *he* happiness for me? What egotism! He only talks about himself! I could never find refuge with a boy as young as that – I could never tell him everything and implore him: "Cure me! Give me what I lack, what I so humbly beg, which would make me like other women." All the women I know talk about *that* so soon as they're alone together – but with words and looks that defile love. So do all the books. And some of them couldn't be more categorical! That one I was reading only yesterday . . .'

She opened a book, on which the printer's ink was still damp, and re-read:

'Their passionate embrace was at once an ecstasy and a

paroxysm of rage. Adila growled like a tigress as she dug her nails into the man's shoulders and their exacerbated glances met like two daggers whetted with sensuality. In a supreme spasm, he felt all his strength dissolve into her, while she, her eyes turned up, soared up in one sweep high above the unknown summits where the Dream becomes one with sensation.'

'Well, that's decisive enough!' concluded Minne, as she closed the book. 'I sometimes wonder what Antoine could have done in his bachelor days to make him so – ignorant.'

Normally, Minne thought little about Antoine. Sometimes she forgot all about him. Sometimes, too, she welcomed him joyfully, as if he were still the brotherly cousin of the old days. But today when he returned home famished, smelling of rosewood and varnish, his cheerful chatter subsided before Minne's obstinate silence – a silence accompanied by a small, pinched mouth and impatient eyebrows.

'What's the matter with you?'

'Nothing.'

There was nothing the matter with her. She was angry with Antoine because of the meeting Jacques had arranged for that afternoon. That boy was getting above himself; he implored her, he imposed himself on her, he wrote letters. True, he was Baron Couderc, but ... 'Much good that'll do him!' thought Minne. 'It might amuse me if I'd stolen him from someone or if I could tell Irène Chaulieu so. But, as far as I'm concerned, whether it's Baron Couderc or the coalman over the road, the result's just the same!'

She would go to the Rue Christophe-Colombe all the same. She would go because she never backed out of anything, even a tiresome duty, and besides, their love-affair was still so new.

In the dining-room, which let in so much light that it made one feel cold, Antoine devoured a plate of Veal Marengo and his newspaper, then gazed ecstatically at his wife. In her tight-fitting, plain dark dress, she looked like a very distinguished sales-girl. He tried, by making conversation, to soften the faraway expression of those black eyes, the torment of his youth, and of that mouth which, in those days, used to lie so crazily and so artistically.

'I've had a good lunch, Minne dear. Did you arrange the menu?'

'Why, of course. As I do every day.'

'It's marvellous! Yet my aunt never taught you anything.'

Minne tossed her head complacently.

'I learnt all by myself. Sauces are out of fashion and complicated *entrées* aren't the thing any more. There are hardly any vegetables at this time of year and, if I didn't take a little trouble, we'd eat as badly here as at the Chaulieus.'

She was being the model little housewife now, folding her hands and enlarging on the difficulties of winter catering. Antoine, half hidden behind his *Figaro*, marvelled at her secretly and chuckled with delight. Minne noticed the sudden fluttering of the newspaper and protested:

'It's too bad! Why are you laughing?'

'Only because I love you so much, my pet.'

He got up and went over and kissed the lovely shining hair through which a narrow black velvet ribbon twisted in and out like a snake. Minne leant her head languidly for a moment against her husband's side.

'You smell of pianos, Antoine.'

'I know I do. It's very healthy, you know. It keeps moths away, this smell of varnish and new wood. Suppose we put a grand piano in each of your wardrobes?'

Minne deigned to laugh, which sent his spirits soaring.

'Up with you! Come and pour out my coffee, darling. I've got to get off early.'

He picked her up in his arms and carried her into the white, flower-papered drawing-room which retained the uninteresting smell of new fabrics, for Minne never received in it and preferred to live in her bedroom and most of all in her dressing-room.

'What are you doing this afternoon, my sweet?'

Minne's face hardened a little, not because she feared any suspicion, but because this second rendezvous, the very day after the first, menaced her peace of mind.

'Some boring shopping. But I'll be home early.'

'Yes, I know what that means! You'll arrive at half past seven, looking as if you'd dropped from the moon and exclaiming: "What? I thought it was only five!" '

Minne shook her head, unsmiling:

'That's highly unlikely.'

In the little ground-floor flat in the Rue Christophe-Colombe, she found the kettle boiling for tea, the fire sinking into red embers and all the vases filled with huge shaggy chrysanthemums. The caviar sandwiches, unwrapped too soon, were curling up like badly pasted-in photographs. Jacques had been there for two hours. He was graver than yesterday and Minne found him changed: there was something sincere and serious about him that did not suit him at all. 'That's just my luck!' she sighed. She hid the ill-humour under a social smile.

'What? So you're here already, my dear Jacques?'

'My dear Jacques' signified that 'yes, he was already here,' and gripped her fingers very tight. 'I could swear he wants to cry,' thought Minne. 'A man in tears ... oh no! Spare me that!'

'Why are you offended with me? Am I late?'

'Yes, but it doesn't matter.'

He helped her to take off her fur, received the little tricorne trimmed with camellias with reverent hands and turned pale when he saw she was wearing the same dress as yesterday and a severe collar in which sparkled the same ruby stud. He felt heartbroken and lost.

'Oh God!' he thought. 'How I love her already! It's terrible, I didn't realize it. Yesterday it was still all right, but today it's all too much for me. All I'm capable of is bursting into tears and making love to her till it kills me. She'll take me for a boor ...'

She turned to him, irritated by his silence.

'I say, Jacques, do let me get a word in edgeways!'

He smiled with a smile that had lost all its gay impertinence.

'Don't laugh at me, Minne, I'm not myself today.'

With an expression of eager concern, Minne went over to the young man sitting in front of her and stroked his soft fair hair.

'But you should have told me so! It would have been so simple to have put it off to another day! You only needed to send me a note.'

This false solicitude rekindled a disquieting light in Jacques' eyes. He got up and said almost harshly:

'Put it off! Send a note! Am I an invalid? It's not a question of flu or a migraine. Do you think I can do without you?'

He had not been able to control himself; he had expressed himself clumsily and Minne was immediately up in arms.

'So, as you can't do without me, I've got to come here at any time you fancy?'

She had not raised her voice but her twitching lips had gone white and she was staring her lover up and down like a frail, menacing animal. He took fright and seized her cold little ungloved hands.

'Good heavens, Minne, we must be mad! What's the matter with me? What am I saying? Forgive me. It's because I love you: all the trouble comes from that. It's because it hurts me so terribly to think of you, you as you were yesterday, and you're going to be again ... Tell me, tell me you *are* going to be as you were yesterday, aren't you? Looking so pale, with your hair all loose and then afterwards, lying tired out on the bed with your slender feet clasped together.'

He went on talking, as he undressed Minne. His kisses, the close embrace of his vigorous, pink young body, the smell of his fair skin, the flash of mysterious beauty which lit up his face at the critical moment, once again revived the hope of a miracle in the depths of Minne's sombre eyes. But, once again, he succumbed alone and Minne, as she watched him lying motionless close beside her, not yet resurrected from a blissful death, analysed in the inmost depths of herself her reasons for beginning to hate him. She ferociously envied this passionate boy's ecstasy, the swooning rapture he did not know how to give her: 'He steals that pleasure from *me*! It's mine, *mine* – it's *I* who should be struck by that divine thunderbolt that flings him prostrate on me! I want that ecstasy – or else that he should stop knowing it through me!'

'Minne!'

The boy, appeased, sighed that name as he reopened his eyes in the coloured dusk of the drawn curtains. He was no longer ill-tempered, he was no longer jealous, he felt happy and amiable as he looked for Minne across the great bed and cajoled her:

'Minne, hurry up and come back. You're being an awful long time!'

As she did not come back, he sat up and remained staring, open-mouthed, when he saw that Minne had her corsets on and was retying the narrow black velvet ribbon in her hair.

'Are you crazy? Surely you're not going?'

'Of course I am.'

'Where?'

'Home.'

'You didn't tell me that your husband . . .'

'Antoine doesn't get back till seven.'

'Then why on earth?'

'I don't want to stay any longer.'

He leapt out of the bed, naked as Narcissus, stumbling over the boots he had flung down anyhow.

'Minne! What have I done to make you leave me? Did I hurt you? Perhaps I hurt you a little?'

She was about to speak, to reply: 'Not even that!' – to tell of her long search and her fruitless infidelities – but a peculiar reticence restrained her. That secret, together with her divagations of long ago, must at least remain her own sad possession.

'No, I'm quite all right. I'm going because I don't want to stay. I've had enough.'

'Enough of what? Of me?'

'If you like. I don't love you enough.'

She dealt him this crashing blow as if she were making a pretty speech, as she drew on her rings. For him, all this was a nightmare . . . or was it a practical joke?

'Minne darling, you're too amusing for words! Never a dull moment with you!'

He laughed, still naked. Minne, with her hands in her muff, stared at him. She hated him. She was certain of that now. Ruthlessly and shamelessly she scrutinized every detail of his person, the face like a tired child's, the mauve shadows under the eyes, the lax, flushed mouth, the chest with its fuzz of golden hair, the lean muscular thighs . . . She hated him. She bent down lower and said softly.

'I don't love you enough to come back. Yesterday, I wasn't sure. The day before yesterday, I knew nothing about it. You didn't know, yesterday, that you loved me. We've both of us made discoveries.'

Then she glided swiftly to the door, so that he should not have time to do her an injury.

Antoine, who was returning home on foot from the Roche-chouart district felt gloomy for two reasons: firstly because it was thawing and the greasy pavements sent up a steamy mist that tasted like a wet dishcloth; secondly because his chief had irritably called him 'a musical instrument maker for mummies'.

He was so absorbed in depressing thoughts that he re-entered the house without making any of his usual noise; he did not sing in the hall or knock the umbrellas hanging up inside the front door off their hooks. He pushed open the door of the drawing-room before anything had announced his arrival and stopped dead, in surprise: Minne was there, asleep on the white, flower-patterned sofa.

Asleep? Why asleep? She had laid her hat on the table, thrown her gloves into a jardinière, and her muff, which had fallen at her feet, looked like a cat crouching in the shadow ... Such disorder was as unlike Minne as finding her dead asleep at this time of day. He went up closer to her: she was asleep with her head against the hard back of the sofa, and some strands of her silvery-gold hair had tumbled down on her shoulder. He leant over her, his heart beating, feeling vaguely frightened and ashamed of being there, as if he were opening a stolen letter. How sad this child he adored looked in her sleep! Her brows were knitted and her relaxed mouth drooped at the corners. Suddenly the delicate nostrils dilated, began to breathe harder ... Was that blind, distressed face about to melt into tears?

'What is changed about her?' Antoine thought with anguish. 'She's no longer the same Minne. Where has she come from, so tired and so unhappy? She looks so desolate in her sleep and I've never felt her so far away from me. Is she going to start lying again?'

It was already a lie, that exhausted sleep, that other face which she never showed him. He recoiled a step, Minne had stirred. Her hands jerked faintly, as dogs' paws do when they run in their dreams, and she suddenly sat bolt upright, looking terrified.

'Is it you? Whatever's this. What are *you* doing here?'

Antoine gazed at her searchingly.

'It's me, Minne. I've just come in. Did you think I was someone else?'

Minne, who had been so pale, flushed crimson to the roots of her hair and took a great gulping breath.

'Thank goodness it's you! I was having such a bad dream!'

Antoine sat down beside her, still riddled with doubt and uneasiness.

'Tell me your bad dream.'

She smiled her feminine, impudent smile and shook her fallen strand of hair.

'No, thank you! I don't want to be frightened all over again!'

'I'd reassure you, Minne darling,' said Antoine, throwing his long arm right round her.

But she escaped, with a laugh, and began to dance about the room to get warm again, to wake herself up and forget the frightening picture she had seen in her dream of the naked body of a fair-haired young man stretched out dead on a red carpet . . .

Today was Sunday, a day that upset the routine of the week and was unlike all other days. On Sundays, Antoine – who assumed that he liked music now that he was engaged on reconstructing the *barbytos* – took Minne to concerts.

Minne could never think why it was that she always felt chillier on Sundays. She arrived at a concert with her teeth chattering and the music did not warm her up in the slightest because she listened too intently. She listened, leaning forward, her hands clasped inside her muff, never taking her eyes off the conductor, as if some gesture of Chevillard's or Colonne's would at last raise the curtain on some mysterious spectacle one divined behind the music, but she never saw ... 'Oh, why, *why* is nothing ever perfect?' sighed Minne. 'You wait and you wait, you feel as if your whole body wanted to burst into tears and ... nothing happens!'

It was a grey Sunday of thawing snow and slush. Minne arrayed herself for it in a grey velvet dress the colour of tarnished silver and a black fox stole. Under her hat, crowned with sombre plumes, her hair capped the nape of her neck like a helmet of polished gold. Standing in her dressing-room, contemplating herself from all angles in a triple mirror, Minne admitted herself satisfied.

'I really look quite like everyone's idea of a society woman.'

Then she went off to plague her husband, for her own perfection made her naturally dictatorial. He dressed in a tiny room, squeezed in behind his study: Minne would not tolerate men's suits, which are dark and rough to the touch, in her own room, or masculine underclothes either. 'If at least,' she said, 'you could put ribbons on pants and flannel waistcoats, so that a cupboard would look pretty when one opened it!'

Antoine was in process of dressing, with the silent speed that resulted from his school training.

'Hurry up, Antoine, hurry up!' scolded the little fairy in silver.

He turned a preoccupied, bearded face, with the black and white eyes of a kindly South American adventurer, towards her:

'Put the links in my left cuff, will you, Minne?'

'I can't, I've got my gloves on.'

'You could take one of them off.'

He did not insist further, but the same preoccupation clouded his brow again. Minne was admiring herself in the tilted mirror of an old pier-glass relegated to this den and which Minne never consulted: there was always something new to be learnt from an unknown looking-glass.

Suddenly she sang in her shrill, pure, little girl's voice:

> *J'ai du di*
> *J'ai du bon*
> *J'ai du dénédinogé,*
> *J'ai du zon, zon, zon,*
> *J'ai du tradéridera;*
> *J'ai du ver-t-et jaune*
> *J'ai du vi-o-let*
> *J'ai de l'orangé!*

Antoine turned round, startled.

'Whatever's that?'

'That? It's a song.'

'Where did you learn it?'

She tried to think, with a finger pressed to her temple and suddenly remembered that her first lover, the young house-surgeon, used to sing this peasant nonsense rhyme in a way that made it sound fantastically obscene. The recollection amused her and she burst out laughing.

'I don't know. When I was little. Perhaps in the kitchen, with Célénie?'

'That surprises me,' said Antoine, more seriously than the occasion warranted. 'I knew Célénie as well as you did.'

Minne waved a careless hand.

'I daresay ... You know it's nearly two o'clock and it's terrible getting a cab on Sunday.'

In the cab, Antoine did not utter a word, his brow puckered with an uneasiness he could not explain. Minne decided to comfort him and give him some sage advice.

'My poor boy, if it takes you two days to get over it every time someone makes a joke about your – what's its name? – *barbytos*, wherever will you get in life? Come on now, there's always bound to be some fly in the ointment and if you never have any worse catastrophes to face ...'

She sighed, sounding so comically motherly and disillusioned, that Antoine's morose humour melted into warm tenderness and by the time they were climbing the steps of the Palais du Châtelet, he had recovered the aggressive pride of any man with an extremely pretty woman on his arm.

'Look, Antoine, there's Irène Chaulieu ... over there in a box with her husband.'

'And with Maugis. Can he be making a pass at *her*?'

'Oh, that means nothing!' said Minne pertly. 'He's making one at me too.'

'No!'

'Certainly! The other night, at the Chaulieus, if I'd been willing.'

'For goodness' sake, not so loud! Your idea of keeping your voice down! So Maugis dared to make suggestions to you?'

'Oh, Antoine, for mercy's sake don't let's have a matrimonial scene in public – and on account of Maugis of all people! He's not worth bothering about. And, anyway, shut up ... here's Pugno coming on to the rostrum.'

He said no more. In his heart, he cared nothing about Maugis. His new uneasiness concerned Minne and Minne alone. He thought – good heavens, he was *certain* – that Minne was not doing anything foolish: all he was afraid of was that she might be beginning to lie again for the pleasure of lying, that she might once again be cultivating that perverse, magical, unknown garden in which she had wandered all her mystery-loving childhood.

'Hullo, there's little Couderc,' he said absent-mindedly.

Only Minne's eyes stirred.

'Where?'

'He's just come into Madame Chaulieu's box. How they're jabbering in that box! You can hear them from here.'

Indeed, Irène Chaulieu was chattering as uninhibitedly as if she were at the Opera. She presented a three-quarter view of herself against the red hangings and her oriental eyelids fluttered to express lassitude, desire and volumptuous acquiescence. Quantities of real, but shabby, lace loaded her shoulders and hung from her sleeves.

'It really *is* true,' whispered Minne, 'that she always looks as if she bought her dresses from the second-hand clothes women in the Rue de Provence!'

She pretended to be picking Irène's get-up to pieces in order to scrutinize Jacques Couderc. How ill that boy looked! And one of his hands kept feverishly jerking his hat up and down. Minne thought contemptuously:

'I loathe these nervous people who can't hide their feelings! The other day it was his knee that had St Vitus's dance; today it's his arm! All those tics mean he's a degenerate!'

She was secretly revenging herself for the faint thrill in the nape of her neck of which she had just momentarily been conscious. Then, with her chin thrust out and her ears all attention, she prepared to give herself up wholly to *Scheherezade*.

Her body swayed to the rhythm of the waves – unleashed trombones crested with a clash of cymbals. A faint smile stretched the corners of her lips when Rimsky-Korsakov carried her away from the ship to the harem, from the shipwrecks to feasts in Bagdad; when, as she emerged from the marvellous clamour of a battle of giants, he plunged her up to the lips in the oriental jam – pistachio-nuts, rose-petals, sticky with sugar and oil of sesame – of a dialogue between the prince and the young princess. Was this overwhelming music going to deliver up to Minne the secret of herself?

Too much sweetness at moments or else the shameless violins, conveying the irresistible impression of the wild whirling dance of a beauty veiled in scarves, made mouths open here and there and gasp an ecstatic 'Ah!'

In Irène Chaulieu's box, an unhappy boy was trying to understand what had happened to him. The music shattered his nerves and when the violins sang piercingly he needed considerable courage not to howl like a dog beside a barrel-organ. The presence of Minne overwhelmed him. She had abandoned him, naked and weak; she had abandoned him, still intoxicated with her, with such cold, measured words, such black, fiercely resolute eyes ... Alas! the story of their love could be written in three lines: he had seen her ... she had attracted him because she was like no one else ... and then she had given herself at once, in silence ...

'How hot it is in here!' sighed Irène Chaulieu. Her fan wafted a heavy, cloying perfume towards Jacques Couderc and he felt sick. Oh, how a drop of lemon verbena would rejuvenate the dusty air! Peeled lemons, leaves you rub to make them yield you their green smell, the freshness of early summer, barley straw just turning yellow – Minne's scent, Minne's hair, Minne's skin. And then her eyes, those black pools where dreams came to drink and see their own reflections mirrored. 'Is it possible that I had all that? And how did I deserve it? And how did I lose it?'

'I say, little Jacques, you look ghastly! Debauchery, pale debauchery? Guilty pleasures? Whatever have you been having done to you? I'd be amused to know, not to mention see!'

He smiled at Irène, longing to kill her, and exaggerated his insolent shortsightedness.

'So young, and already a *voyeuse*?'

Irène stuck up her predatory nose.

'My boy, you have suburban prejudices. And suppose it does amuse me to double my own pleasure by the sight of someone else's? You make me laugh, all of you, setting yourselves up to assign respectable limits to sensual pleasure! My own spirit remains oriental enough, thank heaven, to imagine and embrace the sensuality of all the ages.'

She went on, regardless of all the indignant 'sshes' and did not even hear Maugis grumbling out loud:

'Whatever's the woman been reading since yesterday?'

Jacques Couderc fell silent, discouraged, and the interval came opportunely to allow him to leave the box, to move about and exercise his grief. For a brief moment, he contemplated waiting for Antoine and greeting Minne and frightening her; but a kind of moral torpor prevented him. All the words he was trying to prepare so carefully melted away one by one and, like a coward, he walked down the main staircase and out into the street.

This shameful flight gave Minne great self-confidence during the following days; the consciousness of being, for once, the stronger. In any case, the week of New Year's Day, which disturbed even the calm purlieus of the Place Péreire, kept Minne busy perforce with the cares of boxes of sweets, visits, cards and presents. Her tortuous and capricious but never frivolous mind no longer gave a thought to the brief, sorry love-affair. She bustled about like a sales-girl at Boissier's, drew up lists of visits that had to be paid, slipped Christmas cards into envelopes and resumed the anxious expression of a little girl playing at being a grown-up lady.

'And the d'Hauvilles? Ten to one, you never thought about their little boy.'

'That's true, I forgot him.'

'I was sure you had!'

'And that old witch, Madame Poulestin?'

'Oh bother! Yet another!'

He nodded gloomily.

'Honestly, Antoine, it's a bit much if I've got to be the one who thinks of everything!'

Besides, wasn't it also 'a bit much' having to go tomorrow to see Uncle Paul, that hostile invalid, whom she would have to kiss – actually kiss! – on his boxwood-coloured forehead? Horror! The mere prospect of it put her nerves on edge and she rumpled her hair with both hands.

'What time tomorrow, Antoine?'

'What time what?'

'Uncle Paul, of course!'

'*I* don't know. Two o'clock. Or three o'clock. We've got the whole day.'

'You make me fed up! Good night, I'm going to bed, I can't keep upright any longer.'

She stretched and gave a desperate yawn, suddenly bored with all this frenzied application to social duties, then came and offered a small section of cheek, an ear and some hair for her husband's kiss.

'You're going to bed, my pet? All right, then I'll . . .'

'What?'

'I'll go too.'

She gave him a sidelong, feline glance. There was no doubt about it: Antoine would follow her into her bedroom, into her bed. She hesitated: 'Am I ill? Should I make a scene and sulk? Or go to sleep? That would be difficult...'

It would certainly be difficult, for Antoine was stalking up and down, inhaling her light scent all over the room. She followed him with her eyes. He was tall – rather too tall. He looked awkward in his clothes, but, like most well-built men, nakedness put him at his ease. A nose with a hump in the middle, eyes like an amorous coalheaver's ... 'Well, that's my husband. He's no worse than any other man but ... he's my husband. In short, as regards tonight, I'll get some peace sooner if I consent ...' On this conclusion, which contained the whole philosophy of a slave, she walked slowly up to her bedroom, taking out her hairpins as she went.

Uncle Paul was a hideous sight. His head, which seemed to be carved out of gnarled boxwood, was frightening. It looked like the head of a missionary, who had been partly scalped, partly burnt and partly starved to death in a cage exposed to the sun. He sat shrivelled up in an armchair, in the middle of a whitewashed room, playing hide-and-seek with death, and looked after by a blonde, cowlike nurse. He welcomed his children without speaking, extended a dried-up hand and deliberately drew Minne down towards his bald head, delighted to feel her go rigid and to know that she could have screamed.

He and she understood each other perfectly, behind Antoine's back. Minne, with her black eyes fixed wide open, wished him dead: he silently cursed her every minute, quite unjustly accusing her of making Mamma die of grief and of making his son very unhappy.

She asked for his news in a drawling voice: he found enough breath to compliment her on her silver-grey dress. If they had lived in the same house, no one knows what might have happened.

Today Uncle Paul amused himself by detaining Minne as long as possible.

'It's not New Year's Day every day,' he said, choking.

He deliberately brought on a fit of coughing and prolonged it by breathing very hard. The final nauseating spasms made Minne turn pale and shudder. When he had recovered his breath, he went into minute details about his natural functions and was delighted to catch his daughter-in-law's look of revulsion. Then he gathered up his strength and began a slow discourse on the death of his sister.

This time it was a useless waste of energy: Minne, who felt completely innocent of Mamma's death, listened without remorse, and little by little relaxed sufficiently to put in a word or two, with a sad, tender smile. 'She's very tough!' thought the dying man, indignantly. And, tired of the game, he brought the visit to an end.

Outside, in the stinging, frosty dark, Minne felt like dancing. She gave a coin to a beggar, took Antoine's arm and thought, feeling generous in the joy of escaping: 'If Jacques Couderc were here, upon my word I'd kiss him!'

All the evening she bustled about, chattering, laughing all by herself at nothing. Her dark eyes were restless and sparkling, a charming feverish flush enlivened her pale cheeks. Antoine observed her with a sad attentiveness. At one moment, she broke off laughing to smile, and her face changed. Oh, that smile of Minne's! That provocative, enchanting smile that lifted her cheeks, transformed the curve of her mouth and drew up the corners of her eyelids! For the second time, Antoine was constrained to discover another face on Minne's face, a mask lightly imposed on it by the smile. His heart felt faint and sick, as on the day he had seen her asleep on the sofa. In that anxious sleep which betrayed her, as in this secret, sensual smile in which another woman appeared, Minne had escaped from him. This time, it was only for a flash; for Minne yawned like a cat, clenched her claws on empty air and announced she was going to bed.

Minne could not go to bed straight away. Wrapped in her white monk's robe, she opened her window to 'see the cold'.

She raised her head and the twinkling of the stars surprised her. How they quivered! That big one up there above the house, surely it was going to go out: it must have been hung up in a draught.

Having played long enough at enjoying the cold, Minne shut the window and remained standing against the pane feeling too light-headed, too subtly excited tonight to go to bed. She was seized once again by the absurd, burning conviction that happiness might still burst into her life like a marvellous catastrophe, like a sudden fortune, and that she deserved it, that it was her due. No doubt the man who would make a woman of her bore no mysterious signs, and if she found him, it would be by chance. Chance, in the old days, was called a miracle. More than once, a quarryman, with one blind stroke of his pickaxe had smashed the rock which imprisoned a spring ...

Irène Chaulieu had asked Minne to meet her at the Palais de Glace about five o'clock.

Her 'At Home day' was not enough for the indefatigable little Jewess who considered being alone and doing nothing as illnesses. Every day she gathered together in some tea-room a collection of friends, enemies and former lovers who had remained docile. Her lace trains, edged with sable, frequently swept the long gallery of the Frizt. The Empyrée-Palace and the Astoria reverberated with her piercing voice, which was as audible as a yapping dog's when she thought she was whispering. The old-fashioned Palombin and the discreet Afternoon lost all their quiet on the days Irène Chaulieu booked a table there. Today it was the Palais de Glace. Minne, who was going there for the first time, had put on a plain dark dress like a respectable woman going to her first rendezvous with a lover and a close-fitting sprigged veil which tattooed a white pattern on her delicate, invisible face: only two holes of impenetrable shadow and a pink flower were discernible as her eyes and her mouth.

'Ah! Here's Saint Minne! Where have you come from in that muzzle? Maugis, give this child your seat. How's Antoine? Do have a hot grog: it's as cold as death here. And besides, in Rome one must do as the Romans do. I always drink tea in England, chocolate in Spain, beer in Munich.'

'I didn't know you'd travelled so much,' slipped in Maugis' suave voice.

'An intelligent woman has always travelled a lot, you old drunk!'

Maugis, in a light waistcoat, with his paunch sticking out like a fat hen's, was strutting for Minne's benefit, but she seemed not to notice it. She was looking about her, disappointed, after having summed up with her eyes the guests at this tea party. Not a brilliant lot, today! Irène had brought her sister, a frog-like monster with a hump and almost no legs, impossible to marry off, whom Irène lodged and fed, terrorized and forced into a mute complicity. The regular frequenters of the Chaulieus' salon had nicknamed this deformed duenna 'My sister Alibi'.

Beside Maugis, a dim blue-stocking was sipping a very dark cocktail. 'Beautiful Suzie', the American, was absorbed in a whispered duologue with her neighbour, an Andalusian sculptor with a Christ-like beard. All that could be seen of her was a short thick nape, square shoulders and the short, velvety nose of a sensual animal. Finally there was Irène, badly dressed and in a bad temper. Minne noted with calm pleasure the glaring make-up on her cheeks and lips, the excess of jewellery on her neck and bare hands.

Minne was waiting for Maugis, who was standing behind her, to resume their flirtation. He was brooding over her with eyes whose innocent blue had been tarnished by alcohol and trying to rediscover the sloping line of her shoulders, the pale veined arms, the two touching little salt-cellars, under the severe tailored dress. Patiently, Minne occupied herself in watching the whirling of the skaters. That at least was new, a little dizzying to watch but every minute becoming more enthralling. She caught herself leaning forward following the impetus which made all the skaters bend over like corn in a wind. The light falling from above hid the faces under the shadow of their hats; the scarred rink, dusted with powered ice, cast a snowy reflection upwards. The skates purred and, under their stress, the ice screeched like a pane of glass being cut.

Some very elaborately dressed women brushed Minne's elbow: those were the ones she would have liked to see skating, with all their feathers whirling and their skirts swelling out like spinning tops. But of course those were the ones who did not go down on to the rink.

'Minne, have you seen Polaire?'

'No; what's she like?'

'That's so typical of you! You'll always remain in my mind as the woman who doesn't know Polaire! There, look: she's just going by.'

Two waltzing figures: one of them, slender, with a tightly-cinched waist and a spreading skirt seemed less like a woman than one of those illusions of a vase created by spinning a piece of bent wire. Minne had not seen the waltzer's face – only a pale blot tilted back in a frame of black hair – nor her feet – only a metallic flash, like a flick of a fish's tail in the sun – but she sat spellbound, waiting for the entwined pair of skates to go past again. This time, she felt the draught of the flying skirts and could see the ecstasy on the pale upturned face.

'Can the mere intoxication of whirling so fast on winged feet be enough to give a face that expression of blissful death? That's what I want, too . . . I wonder if I could learn! . . . Imagine spinning and spinning till you die of it, your head thrown back, your eyes shut . . .'

Her name, spoken in an undertone, awakened her.

'Madame Minne looks very absorbed,' Maugis was saying.

'She's thinking of her boy-friend,' retorted Irène Chaulieu.

'Which boy-friend?' Minne condescended to ask.

Irène Chaulieu leant across the table, trailing the tails of her sable stole in the cups: her painted mouth was swollen with the need to talk, to lie, to calumniate, to know all.

'Why, the unluckiest of all of them, little Couderc! No one's talking about anything else, my dear, they know how you received him!'

Minne's eyes twinkled behind the lace veil as she commented inwardly: 'Up to now, it's been he who received me!'

'. . . his poor little face looks a wreck since the day you sent him away . . . to love somewhere else. One meets him in gambling clubs, he loses goodness knows what at the Ferme. In fact, honestly, people would talk less about you two if you'd slept together!'

'Is that a piece of advice?' asked Minne's soft little voice.

'My advice! Anything but! My dear girl, it isn't just because Maugis is here that I assure you *I* don't go about recommending my friends to take up with playboys of twenty-three! All they do is make pests of themselves; either they ask you for money or else they cling to you like burrs and talk of threats, suicides, revolvers and every sort and kind of scandal!'

Minne frowned. Wherever had she seen the white body of a young man stretched out naked on a red carpet? Ah yes, in that bad dream! She shivered under her black fox stole and Maugis, who was staring at her with devout greed, followed the track of the shiver from the nape of her neck to the small of her back.

'Now, now, Maugis, don't get excited!' Irène advised him. 'The ice is having a funny effect on you today!'

'It's my peak hour,' said the journalist. 'You can't imagine how brilliant I am between five and seven!'

Irène's burst of laughter drowned the purr of the skates and interrupted the ecstatic duologue between the beautiful Suzie and the Andalusian sculptor who turned round with a blank, bewildered look, like lovers suddenly woken up. Only the froglike monster, squatting like a Hindu idol, did not smile.

'On the whole ... I'm at my best in the morning,' Irène declared bravely. 'Although, all the same, the afternoon ... or very late at night ...'

Maugis clasped his hands in admiration:

'Oh, rich nature! Is it true that wealth makes one generous?'

She pushed him aside with the tips of her polished nails.

'Wait! Minne hasn't said anything. Minne, it's your turn. I'm waiting to hear the secrets of your love-life. You irritate me, sitting there mum with your hands in your muff.'

Minne hesitated, then put on a mock-childish expression and voice.

'Oh, please don't ask *me* first, I'm only a little girl! I'll speak after everyone else!'

She indicated the Spanish-American couple sitting knee to knee. The American woman had no such inhibitions.

'For me, it depends on who it is,' she declared. 'But all times are equally good.'

'Bravo!' cried Irène. '*You* at least go bravely to your "little death"!'

The beautiful Suzie gave a low laugh and crinkled her cat-like nose:

'Little death? No, it's not that . . . It's more like when the swing goes up too high . . . You feel you've been cut in half and then you come down again and scream "Ha!"'

'Or else: "Ma!"'

'Be quiet, Monsieur Maugis! And then you start all over again.'

'Ah, you start all over again? Congratulations to your . . . swing!'

Irène Chaulieu was nibbling a rose and staring straight in front of her. Fleeting emotions passed over her handsome, Salome-like face.

'Personally,' she began, 'I think you're all egoists. You talk of nothing but *your* pleasure, *your* sensation, as if the other person's were of no importance. The pleasure I give sometimes means more to me than my own.'

'But there's still the way of . . . giving,' interrupted Maugis.

'Be quiet, you! And then the swing – no it's not like that at all. For *me*, it's the ceiling bursting open, a gong sounding in my ears, a kind of . . . of apotheosis which is my right, the advent of my reign over the whole world . . . and then, nothing more! It doesn't last!'

Carried away as she was, Irène Chaulieu seemed to be experiencing a certain genuine sadness.

The scarred, dulled, almost deserted ice-rink cast a pallid reflection on people's faces. A tall strapping young man in a tight-fitting green outfit, with his knitted cap over one ear, was cleaving the rink with the oblique forward thrust of a swimmer.

'He's not bad-looking, that boy ...' murmured Irène. 'What do *you* think, Minne? I'm still waiting for that last word of yours.'

'Yes,' insisted Maugis. 'You owe us the final casting vote in this memorable plebiscite!'

Minne stood up and stretched her veil tight over her chin by thrusting out her lips so that her mouth was as small as a fish's.

'Oh, *I've* nothing to contribute ... You see I've never had anyone but Antoine.'

The uproarious success of her remark slightly disconcerted her. The laughs echoed twice as loud over the empty rink. Women turned round towards their group. The man in the skin-tight outfit recrossed the ice like a ballet dancer with one foot in the air. Followed by the hunchbacked monster, Irène ambled towards the exit, keeping her eye on the green-clad skater.

'He's decidedly not bad-looking, that boy – eh, Minne?'

'Yes ...'

'He's a bit like Boni de Castellane, only more robust. Ah, if one didn't control oneself! But one does control oneself! They're spoilt by infatuated tarts and if you fall for them, the whole of Paris knows it next day!'

She gave a shrug which shook all the tails of her sables, and dismissed the seedy blue-stocking. Then, as Maugis still lingered, she said crossly:

'Come along, you fat drunk, when you've finished licking Minne's gloves!'

The American and the Andalusian sculptor had disappeared, no one knew where or how. Getting more and more ill-tempered, Irène declared, while the commissionaire was calling her car, that 'the beautiful Suzie is off for another go on the swing' and that 'soon no decent woman will want to be seen with her!'

Minne felt her wings sprouting.

Every day for the past week, two o'clock had found her in the Métro, wearing a short skirt, on the way to her skating lesson at the Palais de Glace. The first sessions had been hard. Minne, horrified to feel the ground slipping under her feet like a soapy floor, had squeaked like a trapped mouse or, dumb and wide-eyed with terror, had clutched on to her instructor's arm as if she were drowning. The stiffness was terrible too, and when Minne woke up she complained of 'two new, very painful bones' running all down her shins.

But the wings were sprouting. Now she could glide over the ice in a balanced rhythm, faster and faster till they stopped with a pirouette. Minne let go of the arm of the man in green, clasped her hands in her muff, struck out and glided, erect, with her feet together.

But what she wanted was to waltz like Polaire, to lose all sense of the real world, to turn pale and die, to become the spiral of paper twirling in the hot air above a lamp, the ribbon of smoke twined round the wrist of a smoker absorbed in work.

She tried to waltz and abandoned herself to the arm of the strapping young man in the knitted cap, but the charm did not work; the man smelt of saveloys and whisky. Nauseated, Minne escaped from him and glided alone, first with her arms down, then, with a still timid gesture, raising her hands in the attitude of a Javanese dancer.

She worked every day with the pointless persistence of an ant hoarding up straws. It was an amusing distraction from her melancholic idleness and the exercise brought colour into her pale cheeks. Antoine was pleased.

Today, Minne's obstinate fervour was redoubled. It was doubtful if she so much as even noticed that, outside, March was softening the buds and deepening the blue of the sky, that a puny spring was intensifying the scent of twopenny bunches of flowers, withering mignonette, fading violets, jonquils from Nice that smelt of mushrooms and orange-blossom.

Minne glided over the almost empty rink, striped the ice with the sound of a diamond on a window-pane and suddenly turned short, leaning forward like a swallow – one more stroke and her skate would have touched the barrier.

Without seeing it, she had knocked against an elbow leaning on it, so she turned round, muttering:

'Sorry!'

The man leaning on the barrier was Jacques Couderc. The sight of that humble livid face and those gloomy eyes following her suddenly intoxicated her with inexpressible rage.

'How dare he? It's abominable! He's come to show me how pale he is, like a beggar exhibiting his stump, and his eyes say: "Look how thin I'm getting!" Well, let him get thin! Let him melt away! Let him disappear altogether so that at last I'll be spared the sight of that creature ... that creature!'

She whirled round on the ice like a panic-stricken bird imprisoned in a room, determined nevertheless not to give in and leave the place. It was he who gave in and left.

But this time her victory left her somewhat exhausted, and her slender knees were trembling. She had made up her mind. Since Jacques refused to tear himself away from her, let him die! She blotted him out of her life, once again the cruel little queen who, in her childish fantasies, handed out poison and knives to a whole imaginary people.

The next day, Minne woke up as if she had to catch an early train, and dressed with decisive haste. During lunch, Antoine received curt remarks, hurled at his innocent head like missiles. She tapped her foot on the carpet, followed every one of her husband's movements, wondering: 'Will he ever go?'

He was thinking of going. But, before actually doing so, he stood in front of the mantelpiece, uneasily studying his good-natured brigand's face in the glass and clutching his beard in both hands.

'Minne, suppose I had my beard shaved off?'

She stared at him for a second, then burst into such a shrill and insulting laugh that it hurt Antoine to hear it.

One night during his urgent, hasty love-making she had laughed in that intolerable way because the switch of the electric bell hanging by the bed was knocking against the wall with a regular tick-tock like an erotic metronome. It was of that hateful night that Antoine was thinking as he gazed at Minne. She had laughed so hard that two bright little tears trembled on her fair lashes and the corners of her mouth quivered as if she had been sobbing.

Something hard separated them. He wanted to say to her: 'Don't laugh! Be sweet and childish as you sometimes are. Don't be so elusive, so distant; show some indulgence in your consciousness of being superior to me. Don't be eternally criticizing me with your unfathomable dark eyes! You think I'm a fool because I deliberately behave like one. If I could, I'd make myself still more of a fool so that I could do nothing but love you unthinkingly, with none of the exquisite suffering that your disdain and your very dissimulation have such power to inflict on me.'

But he said nothing and went on mechanically holding his beard in both hands.

Minne stood up and shrugged her shoulders.

'All right then, cut your beard off! Or don't cut it off! Or else cut off half of it! Have yourself shaved like a poodle! But for goodness' sake do something and get a move on because it's frightful to see you standing there like a statue!'

Antoine flushed. Her rudeness took him back to his youth. He thought: 'It's lucky for her at this moment that she's my wife. Because if she were only my cousin, she'd jolly well get something!' And he went off stoically, without kissing his wife.

As soon as she was alone, she rushed to the bell.

'My hat and gloves, quick!'

Out in the street, she was so keyed up with excitement that she ran. Oh, how beautiful life was as soon as a glimmer of danger enhanced it! At last, at last! One glance at that little Couderc's livid face, then that squeamish sensation in her stomach and that trembling in her knees had warned her: this was the dawn of a peril, of some potential, perhaps still unconscious menace ... A peril great enough to fill the desert of her life, to take the place of happiness and love – ah, what a hope! She ran and did not stop to compose her face and recover her breath until she was on the very doorstep of the Palais de Glace. Then, making a studied entrance, she descended to the rink with one hand on the arm of the man in the green costume.

'Would you do up my bootlace, please?'

She bent over, revealing her slim, neat ankle and a little of her calf ... 'Marvellous legs, like a page's ...' Straightening herself up, she struck out on the ice, her eyes vague and her lips set in the fixed smile of an acrobat. She knew that he was there, leaning on the barrier. She did not need to look at him. She could see him in the depths of herself, she could have unerringly drawn all the shadows, all the hollow lines that the progress of the poison had traced on that wasted childish face. She glided proudly over the ice, in a fever of excitement, thinking rapturously: 'If he accosts me, is he going to kiss my hand or kill me?'

The thrilling game went on and on. 'I won't be the first to leave,' Minne swore to herself, her whole being tensed up for the fight. The arena was filling with people. The onlookers concentrated much attention on Minne, who, though she was growing pale and breathless, lost none of her grace. The other was still there. For a moment she went and leant upright against the barrier, with her arms crossed. The other was sitting opposite her, with a hot grog in front of him, waiting. She realized that it was late, that Antoine would come home and be anxious, but if she left now the other would waylay her at the exit. She imagined the tears, the supplications that would turn into threats.

'My profound respects, Madame! I would prostrate myself at your feet, were they not shod in skates!' Whoever had spoken in her dream? Minne recognized that soft, muffled voice. She turned and looked at the speaker with eyes like a sleep-walker's and slowly remembered him as if from some very long time ago.

'Ah, of course! . . . How d'you do, Monsieur Maugis.'

He kissed her glove; she studied his broad, bumpy skull, his short nose, typical of spontaneous and violent characters, his blue eyes that had once been clear and his mouth that was like a big sulky child's.

'You're tired, little lady?'

'Yes, a little . . . I've skated a lot.'

'The selfishness of youth! Has that little Couderc been making you waltz to death again?'

Minne folded her arms, and declared emphatically:

'I've never skated with Monsieur Couderc.'

Maugis did not raise an eyebrow.

'I knew that.'

'Oh?'

'Yes, I knew it. Only it delights me to hear you say it. Are you going? You'll let me see you into a cab, won't you?'

She accepted the offer and made herself pleasant, on account of the *other* who had stood up and thrown some money on the table. She stopped still, he stopped still. As she was looking for the nearest exit, she saw Jacques Couderc make three steps to the left at the same time as she did, then three steps to the right.

What an amusing game – just like an English pantomime! The clowns who make people laugh so much have those flour-white faces and that comical, corpse-like stiffness.

'Let's get out,' said Minne, very loud.

The puppet on the other side of the rink fell into step behind the two of them. Deciding to risk all, Minne leant towards Maugis, brushed him with her shoulder and turned her face to his, laughing. A thrill of pleasure and hope rippled all down her spine ... 'Let it come, whether it's a knife or a bullet or an iron bar on the back of my neck,' she implored under her breath. 'I don't care what, but at least let something come, something horrible enough or merciful enough to kill me on the spot!'

By the cloakroom, she stopped abruptly and turned around. The pale boy who was following them at a distance stopped too.

'Monsieur Maugis, I won't be a minute, I'll take off my skates and meet you here. Would you be kind enough to call me a cab?'

While the critic was hurrying off eagerly, running with a fat man's short, light step, the two lovers remained alone and motionless among the crowd of strangers. The blazing fury of Minne's eyes defied Jacques Couderc and overwhelmed him, calling on him to do and dare. But suddenly the somnambulistic thread that tied him to her seemed to snap. His body went limp and he slunk away.

Outside, a spring twilight hazed the avenue; a mauve dusk, pricked with yellow lights. The air was so moist and caressing that it felt like damp petals brushing against one's cheek. So much sweetness came as a shock to Minne's tense nerves and she swallowed a great gulp of the warm breeze with a shuddering sigh.

'It makes one feel like that, doesn't it?' Maugis replied to that sigh. 'Just look at the green of that sunset – it gives me the blues!'

'How mild it is. Did you call a cab, Monsieur Maugis?'

'Are you very set on your four-wheeler? All the ones going past either have villainous-looking drivers or look like horse-boxes with luggage rails.'

'On the contrary, I'd far rather walk home.'

And, without waiting, she quickened her pace and walked on in silence.

'Ah, little lady,' panted her companion. 'This is one of the moments when I regret Irène Chaulieu.'

'Why?'

'Because she's short. Six inches of legs and you come straight away to her neck. By the side of her I am of noble stature, a tall dashing young man. Whereas with you – we look like something in a fable: "Once upon a time, a bulldog loved a greyhound ..." But at home I regain all my advantages! I am, to be perfectly frank with you, a five-to-seven man, an indoor man, an expert post-lovemaking conversationalist. (Goodness, here's the Rue de Balzac already! By the time we get to the Étoile I shall have nothing left to confess to you!) I am, as I was saying, the man who inspires confidence, the man who receives confidences and never returns them. I give good advice and I praise. Do I have to add that I make iced drinks and tea, am an expert lady's maid and ...'

'And that you never talk about yourself?' interrupted Minne maliciously.

'Chamfort said: "To talk about oneself is to make love."'

'Did Chamfort really say that?'

'More or less. His was not a demanding nature.'

'It certainly wasn't!'

'We're all like that, we celebrated authors, pretty little lady. A little wilted, but so much charm! And if you'd like ...'

'If I'd like what?'

She stopped at the corner of the pavement and leant towards him, coquettish and accessible. Maugis saw her teeth gleam and searched vainly for her eyes under the brim of the large hat.

'Well – and this isn't just the usual old joke – at home I really do have quantities of Kakemonos, Sakie-Mounis and Kamasutras ...'

'Whatever's all that?'

'Japanese painters, of course! Yes we have enough of them, I assure you, to keep us occupied for a whole week of respectable visits. Will you come?'

'I don't know ... Perhaps ... Yes ...'

'But no nonsense, you know! I'm a serious man! You swear to be good?'

She laughed, promised nothing, and left him, blowing him a kiss with her fingertips.

'Ah, the pretty kid!' sighed Maugis. 'To think, if I'd got married, I might perhaps have had a daughter like that!'

When Minne arrived, out of breath, Antoine was having dinner. He was sitting at the table, eating his soup. There was no doubt about it; he was having dinner. Minne could not believe her eyes. There was no sound in the dining-room but the irritating clatter of the spoon on the plate. At every movement of Antoine's arm, the polished belly of the copper lamp reflected a monstrous hand and the tip of a grotesque nose.

'What? You're having dinner? Whatever time is it then? Am I late?'

He shrugged his shoulders.

'Always the same old story! Of course you're late! Are you ever anything else? The Palais de Glace would have to catch fire for you to be home in decent time!'

Minne realized that this was a 'scene', the first worthy of that name. She was going to do nothing to avoid it. She pulled the long pins out of her hat, violently, as if she were pulling so many daggers out of their sheaths, and sat down, facing the danger.

'You should have come and fetched me. Then you could have spied on me at your ease!'

'Except that one's never at ease when one's spying on someone!' Antoine rashly let slip.

Minne leapt to her feet, indignant.

'Ah! You admit it! You do spy on me! That's something new – and flattering!'

He made no reply and crumbled his roll on the tablecloth.

Yes, he did spy on her. Minne, with her mind elsewhere, had not paid sufficient attention to Antoine for some time. He had changed; he talked and ate less and slept little as a gnawing anxiety slowly penetrated his consciousness. The anxiety had a triple visage. Minne's smile, then that tormented sleep, then that little Hecate's insulting laugh superimposed themselves in Antoine's mind and engraved on it the mysterious face of an unknown woman, a stranger.

'I've spent plenty of time on it,' he thought with sad irony.

He had taken photos of Minne at all ages to the office in his brief-case so as to compare them at leisure. In one she was seven years old, with a pointed face like a thin kitten's. Another showed her at twelve, with long ringlets, and, already, what eyes! 'I must have been an idiot not to be disquieted by such eyes!' And there was one where she looked stiff and awkward and her mouth was sad – that was the year when she had been found in a faint by the front door, with her hair full of mud.

'Yes, yes, I've been an idiot and I still am! But she's mine, mine and in the end I'll . . .' But he did not know where to begin and, with a young man's clumsiness, opened his investigation by making a scene.

His tormentor confronted him, serious and fierce. What, again, was this curled-up lip, white with anger? Yet another unknown aspect of this face of which he thought he knew every detail up to the pearly mauve of the eyelids and the delicate branches of the veins? Was she going to come back every day with some change in her looks that shattered his peace of mind?

'Aren't you eating?'

'No. You have such an extraordinary way of giving people an appetite that I shall need time to get used to it.'

'That's right, blame me,' Antoine raged inwardly. 'She goes off goodness knows where while I'm slaving away at the office and it's *she* who's going to scold *me*! What a fool of a husband I've been up to now!'

'So I mustn't say a word?' he shouted. 'You can go off for entire days on end, I don't know with whom, I don't even know where, and if I dare to make a remark, Mademoiselle goes off into . . .'

'Excuse me, *Madame*!' she interrupted coldly. 'You forget that we're married.'

'God in heaven, no, I don't forget it! Things have got to change and we're going to see . . .'

Minne got up and folded her table-napkin.

'What are we going to see, if it's not an indiscreet question?'

Antoine made prodigious efforts to keep calm and pricked the tablecloth with the tip of his knife. His beard trembled and a great throbbing vein stood out across his equine nose. Minne slowly and deliberately straightened up a quivering fern in the épergne.

'We're going to see!' he exploded. 'We're going to see why you're no longer the same!'

'The same as what?'

She stood erect facing him, her hands flat on the table. He stared at that attentive face, that delicate three-cornered chin, those indecipherable eyes, that silvery hair.

'The same as before, of course. Hell, I'm not blind!'

She remained in the same defiant pose, thinking: 'He knows nothing. But he's going to become tiresome.' She knew that one caress would bring him to heel. She had only to put an arm round his shoulders and draw him to her and he would cling to her in a passion of shame and remorse. But she would not stretch her hand out towards her husband. This sudden awakening of Antoine's, like the pursuit of little Baron Couderc who was on her track but had not yet become menacing, were things that she registered passively, as signs of her fate.

Antoine was chewing a violet and gazing into the polished belly of the lamp. The stress of his thoughts and his concentration on the growing pain inside him made him hunch his neck and thrust up his lower jaw. Had not Minne seen that brutelike face somewhere else in the far distant past? The tribe that her childish dreams had idolized had abounded in men with short necks, underhung jaws and low foreheads almost concealed under rough manes.

Minne's very faint sigh had disturbed the silence. Antoine got up, having eaten almost nothing, and went off to take refuge in the drawing-room, where he flung himself down on the sofa where Minne had lain in her guilty sleep. A newspaper was lying on it: he opened it and flicked over the pages with an exaggerated rustling.

'In Manchuria ... They can all go to hell, the whites and the blacks! ... What about the theatres? *Scandal at dress-rehearsal* ... Nation of idlers that we are ... *Young lady of highest social standing (References furnished) seeks marriage ... Cabinet Camille, investigations of all kinds undertaken. Private enquiries of delicate nature a speciality* ... Dirty blackmailing racketeers!'

He felt suddenly tired, lonely and unhappy. 'I am unhappy!' he muttered under his breath, wishing he could repeat those three words out loud so that the sound of his voice might make him pity himself still more and dissolve into soothing tears.

A sound of nibbling came from the dining-room; through the half-open door Antoine could see his wife sitting sideways on the edge of the table. Minne was pecking about in a fruit-dish and crushing almond shells.

'She's had dinner!' thought Antoine. 'She's had dinner, so she doesn't love me!'

He decided from now on to cultivate silence and dissimulation, and picked up his newspaper again.

'Cabinet Camille – private enquiries of delicate nature ...'

Minne, can you grant me an interview one day this week, say tomorrow? If you do not wish to come to my flat, you could arrange to meet me at the British: before four o'clock there is never anyone there.

Jacques

'What a stupid letter!' Minne said to herself, shrugging her shoulders. 'He writes like a shop-assistant, that little Couderc.'

She re-read: 'Minne, can you grant me an interview ...' and remained pensive, her forefinger between her sharp teeth. The very clumsiness of that letter was disquieting, so was the stiffness of the handwriting and the absence of any polite or affectionate formula. 'Suppose I asked Maugis' advice?' At this fantastic idea she broke into her audacious smile. She paced nervously about her bedroom, then drummed on the window-pane. A chestnut bud was brushing against it, swollen and pointed like a flower-bud. The faint breeze which smelt of rain and spring lifted the net curtain. An aimless despair overwhelmed the heart of this lonely child whose frigidity kept her unfairly and absurdly pure after her lapses from virtue and who was searching among men for her unknown lover.

She touched them, then forgot them, as a bereaved mistress might search a battlefield, turning over the dead men, staring at their faces, and then rejecting them and saying: 'It is not he.'

'Monsieur Maugis?'

'He's gone out, Mademoiselle.'

Minne had not foreseen that.

'You don't know when he'll be back?'

'His habits are so irregular that it is quite impossible to say, Mademoiselle.'

Startled, 'Mademoiselle' looked up at the man who had spoken and realized that his clean-shaven face was not that of a manservant. She hesitated.

'Can I leave a note?'

Without saying anything, the clean-shaven young man put out the necessary writing materials on the hall table. He moved as nimbly as a dancer, swaying his hips.

'Dear Monsieur Maugis, I was passing by so I looked in.'

Writing did not come easily to Minne. Her volatile imagination created pictures in swift, trenchant strokes, which needed no assistance from words and she found writing a slow and tedious business.

'*Dear Monsieur Maugis, I was passing by so I dropped in* ... And that creature standing over me all the time! Is he afraid I'm going to steal some writing-paper?'

A door opened and a voice she knew, the voice of an alcoholic young girl, sounded sweetly on Minne's ears.

'Hicksem, do show Madame into the drawing-room. Dear lady, you must excuse the strict orders I have to give to protect my austere solitude.'

Maugis squeezed in his plump paunch to allow Minne to pass. As she entered a long room furnished in fumed oak, she was dazzled by a flood of yellow light.

'Oh, it's all yellow!' she exclaimed gaily.

'Why yes! Sunshine within the reach of all, Provence in your own home! I stuck up two hundred francs' worth of buttercup-yellow gauze. And all for whom? For you alone.'

He pointed dramatically to the yellow curtains hung over the windows. Minne's golden eyelashes fluttered. She remembered the sunbaths in which she had warmed her thin naked body as a little girl in the bedroom of the Dry House ... the old house with the creaking skeleton, the orchard of bluish grass where she used to run about with Antoine, the scene of their brother-and-sister idyll. But wherever was the pink branch of the bignonia which used to tap on the panes with its tubular flowers?

Slightly hallucinated, she turned to Maugis as if to ask him, then fell silent as she noticed the presence of the clean-shaven young man who had opened the door to her. Maugis understood.

'Hicksem, haven't you any shopping to do in the neighbourhood?'

'Yes, certainly,' replied the other, without his shifty eyes betraying anything more than polite indifference.

'Good. As it happens, I've run out of matches. There's a marvellous little shop on the Left Bank which sells them at two sous a box: you see what I mean? Bring me back a box as a sample. God be with you, Signor! See you tomorrow morning!'

The young man bowed, undulated, and disappeared.

Minne was inquisitive. She asked:

'Who's that?'

'Hicksem.'

'What?'

'Hicksem, my private secretary. He's Swiss. He's charming, isn't he?'

'Do you want me to say so?'

'I insist that you do. He's an invaluable boy. He's very well-dressed and that always impresses creditors. And besides, he's queer, thank heaven, as well as getting his clothes in London.'

Minne raised startled eyebrows. What! Was this fat Maugis . . . But he mockingly reassured her:

'No, my child. You've misunderstood me. With Hicksem, my mind's at rest. I can receive one woman friend, two women friends, three women friends all at once or one after the other without being tormented by wondering: "The next time she comes, will it be for me or for my secretary's five-and-twenty summers?" Sit down here by this azure vase which your hair sets off so enchantingly.'

He installed her in the hollow of an armchair and brought up a table on which some lilies-of-the-valley trembled. Minne sat down, disconcerted at finding Maugis so friendly. She was astonished, and showed it. Maugis gave a kindly smile.

'Were it not for my incorrigible vanity, charming little lady, I should think, from the look of you, that you'd come to the wrong flat.'

She passed her hand over her eyes, as if she were not quite awake yet.

'Wait! It feels odd, being here.'

Maugis puffed out his chest and bridled, giving himself a double chin.

'Oh, you can go ahead! I know that "I've got such a charming place" – I like to hear people say so.'

'Yes, it's charming . . . but it doesn't suit you.'

'Everything suits me!'

'No, I mean . . . I didn't imagine the place you lived in would look like this.'

She kept her hands clasped and wriggled her shoulders as she spoke, like a frail animal with its paws tied together. Maugis admired her so much that he had not thought of touching her. A silence passed between them, separating them. Minne felt a vague embarrassment, an uneasiness which she expressed by saying:

'It's nice, your home.'

'Yes, isn't it? All the ladies make complimentary remarks about it. Come and look!'

He got up, tucked Minne's arm under his and was moved to feel it so slim and warm against him.

'For good children I have this doll that Ajalbert brought me back from Batavia. Have a look.'

He pointed to a stand on which was mounted the most savage female divinity ever created by a sculptor of Javanese puppets. She was dressed in tawdry red finery and the narrow, rouged lips in her painted face were smiling, while the long eyes retained a volptuous gravity, an ironic serenity which struck Minne.

'She looks like someone . . . like a man I used to know.'

'A gigolo?'

'No . . . He was called Curly.'

'It's one of my pseudonyms,' declared Maugis, stroking his bald pink pate.

Minne threw back her head and burst out laughing, then stopped short because Maugis was staring greedily at the enchanting line of her throat revealed by her raised chin. Coquettishly, she disengaged her arm.

'Let's go and look at something else, Monsieur Maugis.'

'Please don't call me "Monsieur"!'

'What should I say?'

The fat novelist lowered his eyes modestly.

'My name's Henry.'

'Why, so it is. Everyone knows that, because you sign your

work Henry Maugis. It's funny, one never thinks of you being called Henry, without the Maugis.'

'I'm no longer young enough to have a first name.'

There was a genuine melancholy in his voice. Something new blossomed in Minne's heart, something which as yet had no name in her thoughts and which is called pity. 'That poor man, who will never, never be young again!'

She leant against Maugis' shoulder and smiled at him, generously offering him her delicate, unlined face, her dark eyes, to which the yellow window gave a glint of gold, the shining clear-cut line of her teeth. It was the first alms Minne had ever given disinterestedly and the over-proud beggar accepted only half of the offered gift, for he kissed the downy cheek and the lowered screen of the eyelashes but did not bite the submissive little mouth.

Minne began to be disconcerted. This adventure contradicted all her previous experiences for hitherto she had never set foot in a bachelor's flat without – after the first grateful cry of 'You've come at last!' – being embraced, undressed, possessed and disappointed, all before it struck half-past five. This man of forty would have offended her by his restraint, had he not disarmed her by a fundamental soft-heartedness which betrayed itself in his careful gestures and in his eyes, which so quickly misted over.

And then Minne was baffled as to what attitude to adopt. The men (Antoine included) who invited her to lie down on a bed could be treated as docile cousins or as companions in vice. She could order them imperiously, as she tidied her dishevelled hair: 'If you don't button up my boots for me, I won't come again!' or 'I don't care if it *is* raining, go and get me a cab!' With Maugis, she would not dare ... the difference in their ages both humiliated and comforted her. Fancy sitting chatting, fully dressed, with a man in his own home! Fancy not immediately taking down her hair in front of him, releasing it from the black velvet ribbon, and letting it loose in a silvery flood!

Maugis went on talking, showing her rare bindings and an ivory Nativity, 'fifteenth-century German, my child!' which stood side by side with an obscene faun, rusted green by the earth in which it had slept for a thousand years. She laughed and turned away, holding one hand like a fan over her eyes.

'Imagine – for a thousand years! For a thousand years this little goat-foot has been thinking of the same thing, without weakening! Ah, they don't make them like that any more.'

'Thank heaven,' sighed Minne, with such heartfelt conviction that Maugis gave her a suspicious sidelong glance.

'Could that poisonous Irène Chaulieu have, by any chance, told the truth? Could Minne not be interested in men?'

He replaced the faun in front of the Nativity and pulled down his light waistcoat which was too tight and wrinkled over his stomach.

'Is it a long time since you've seen Madame Chaulieu?'

'At least a fortnight. Why do you ask me that?'

'No particular reason: I thought you were intimate friends.'

'I haven't got any intimate women friends.'

'So much the better.'

'What's that got to do with you? And, besides, I'd really hardly go and choose Madame Chaulieu for an intimate friend. Have you ever looked at her hands?'

'Never between meals: it upsets my digestion.'

'They look as if they'd been messing about with goodness knows what!'

'Because that's just what they have been doing.'

'Exactly. They frighten me. They must be infectious.'

Maugis kissed Minne's pretty tapering white hands.

'My child, how delighted I am to see you have such scruples about hygiene! Rest assured that here you will find the latest refinements in modern antisepsis. Thymol and lysol shall fume at your feet like choice incense. Suppose you remove that hat? Lewis is a great man, certainly, but you look like a lady paying a call. The fox as well ... You see, I'm putting all that, together with the gloves, on the little table – our fashion department.'

Minne was amused and laughed, feeling relaxed. 'Little Couderc would never have amused me like that and made me forget why I had come here,' she thought. 'All the same it must end in that!'

And – since she had come for that, hadn't she? – she went on methodically undressing. She unbuckled her supple leather belt, let her skirt slide to her feet, followed by her white petticoat. And before the dumbfounded Maugis had even had time to express the desire for it, there was Minne standing up, totally unselfconscious, in her knickers – those narrow, unfashionable knickers that fitted tight to her elegant thighs, leaving her perfect knees free.

'Good heavens!' gasped Maugis, his face crimson. 'Is all that for me?'

She replied with a mischievous grimace and sat down on the sofa, waiting. The scantiness of her attire appeared to cause her not the slightest embarrassment nor was there anything immodest in her gestures. The yellow light played on the sloping line of her shoulders and gave a greenish tinge to her pink satin corsets. A string of pearls, no bigger than rice-grains, glistened over the two touching little salt-cellars.

Maugis, as he sat down beside her, coughed and turned purple in the face. Minne's lemon verbena scent wafted towards him in waves and moistened his tongue with a taste of acid-drops. So many charms offered to him and which he had not yet dared to ask for were not, however, enough for him. Confronted with this calm, cold child, he was embarrassed. There was an absent-minded air about her, an almost deferential smile which suggested a little girl trained to prostitution by an infamous mother.

Minne had undone her four pink suspenders. The corsets and knickers were added to the other things in the fashion department. With a chilly little shrug Minne slipped off the shoulder-straps of her chemise and, naked to the waist, thrust out her chest, proud of her small, wide-apart breasts. In her desire to appear 'more of a woman', she tried to make them stand out as much as possible by stiffening her torso as she offered them to Maugis.

He cautiously touched the flowers of those virginal breasts and Minne did not shiver. He clasped one arm round a waist which yielded obediently, without any rebellious tensing and equally without any flattering shudder.

'Little icicle,' he whispered, pulling her down across his knees. Lying there on her back, Minne put both her arms round his neck like a sleepy baby waiting to be carried off to bed. Maugis kissed the golden hair, suddenly touched by the passivity of this naked child who laid her head on his shoulder resignedly rather than affectionately. What chance, what caprice had thrown this slender body into his lap?

'My poor lamb,' he whispered, as he kissed her. 'You don't love me a bit, do you?'

She uncovered her pale face and looked up at him with two grave eyes.

'Oh, but I do. More than I thought.'

'To delirium?'

She laughed maliciously, twisted like a snake and rubbed her delicate skin against the tweed of his waistcoat and the hard horn buttons.

'No one's driven me to delirium yet.'

'Is that a reproach?'

He picked her up like a doll and she felt herself being carried off to more secret recesses. She clutched on to him, suddenly terrified.

'No, no! Please! Please! Not straight away!'

'What's the matter? Headache? Feeling ill?'

Minne was breathing in great gasps, her eyes closed and her small breasts heaving. She seemed to be struggling to tear something very heavy out of herself. Then she choked and a flood of tears abated the violent trembling that Maugis could feel running all through her. Great bright tears that hung in round drops for a moment on the end of the fair, lowered lashes before rolling down her cheeks without wetting them ...

For the first time, Maugis felt his long experience of very young women fail him.

'Really, now, this is quite extraordinary! Come, come

now, my child! . . . Honestly, I'm at my wits' end! Whatever must we look like, I ask you! There, there . . .'

He carried her back to the couch, laid her on it, rearranged the chemise that draped Minne's hips like a loincloth, and stroked the soft tangled hair. His plump hand gently dried the hasty tears, then slid a cushion under the bare back of his strange conquest.

Minne calmed down and smiled, still sobbing a little. She looked round at this sunlit room as if she were just waking up. Against a wall of a pleasant shade of green, a marble bust writhed its voluptuous, muscular shoulders. A Japanese kimono, flung over the back of a chair, was more beautiful than a bunch of flowers.

Minne's eyes went from discovery to discovery till they reached the man sitting beside her. So this fat Maugis, with his old soldier's moustache, was something better than a whisky-sponge and a woman-chaser? There he was, looking genuinely upset, with his tie all askew! He was not handsome, he was not young, and yet it was to him that she owed the first joy of her loveless life, the joy of feeling cherished, protected, respected.

With a shy, daughterly gesture, she laid her small hand on the hand that had tended her, the hand that had just pulled up her chemise when it was slipping off.

Maugis sniffed and said in a louder voice:

'Better now? Not nervous any more?'

She shook her head.

'A little white port? Oh, a port for children: sweet as sugar!'

She drank it in small sips, pausing between each, while he stoically admired her. The transparent linen half veiled the pink flowers of her breasts and revealed a little of her tapering thighs above the bronze stockings. He longed with all his heart and all his senses to take this child whose face was so serious under her silvery hair! But he felt that she was frail and lost, wretched as a stray animal, frightened of sex, sick with some secret that she did not want to tell.

She held out her empty glass.

'Thank you. It's late. You're not angry with me?'

156

'No, darling. I'm an old gentleman, with no resentment and no vanity.'

'But . . . I wanted to tell you . . .'

She was slowly putting on her corsets, with fumbling, inattentive hands.

'I wanted to tell you . . . that . . . I would have disliked it just as much, and even more, with any other man.'

'Really and truly?'

'Yes, really and truly!'

'Is it that you're delicate? Or ill? Or frightened?'

'No, but . . .'

'Come on! Tell your old Nanny Maugis all! You don't like it, eh? I bet Antoine isn't much of an expert.'

'Oh, it isn't only Antoine's fault,' Minne replied evasively.

'And . . . the other one? Little Couderc?'

At that name, Minne tossed her head so contemptuously that Maugis thought he understood.

'He bores you as much as that, that schoolboy?'

'Bores is too mild a word,' she said coldly.

She finished fastening her four suspenders, then stood up and faced him squarely and resolutely.

'I've slept with him.'

'Ah, I'm delighted to hear it!' said Maugis gloomily.

'Yes, I've slept with him. I've slept with him and with three other men, counting Antoine. And not one of them, not one of them, you hear, has given me a little of that pleasure that left them lying, half dead, beside me! Not one of them has loved me enough to look in my eyes and see my disappointment, to see that I was hungry and thirsty for what *I'd* glutted *them* with!'

She was shouting and beating her breasts with her clenched fists. She was theatrical, but touching too. Maugis stared at her, listening avidly.

'Then never . . . never . . .?'

'Never!' she repeated plaintively. 'Is there a curse on me? Is there something mysteriously wrong with me physically? Is it that I've only met brutes?'

She was almost dressed, but her dishevelled hair still hung

loose, flung like a mane over one shoulder. She stretched out beseeching hands to Maugis.

'Wouldn't *you* be willing to try . . .'

She dared not add more. Her fat friend leapt to his feet with the agility of a young man and seized her by the shoulders.

'My poor love! Now *I'm* the one who'll say: "Never!" I'm an old man, very much in love with you, but an old man! All you see now is just the usual fat Maugis with his jovial paunch and his eternal light waistcoat, Maugis in uniform. But, now I know how ignorant you are, to let you see the beast there is under the light waistcoat and the pleated shirt, let you carry away the memory of a disillusion worse than the others, of lecherousness without grace or youth . . . no, my darling, never! Do me only one favour – give me a little credit for resisting the temptation, and then . . . and then, be off with you! Antoine might be getting anxious.'

She made an attempt at a mischievous smile.

'He'd be quite wrong.'

'True, my Minon. But everyone can't know that I'm a saint.'

'All the same, if you wanted . . . Now, I'm not frightened any more.'

Maugis gathered all Minne's hair up in his hand and let it run through his fingers against the light for the pleasure of seeing it ripple.

'I know that. But I'd be the one who wouldn't have a dry stitch left.'

She did not insist, but began hurriedly to put up her hair, seeming to be gazing into the sombre depths of her thoughts. Maugis handed her one by one the little amber-coloured combs, the black velvet ribbon, her hat, her gloves.

There she was, just as she had been when she arrived; and all the fat man's sensuality cried out with regret and ferociously scoffed at him. But Minne, ready to leave, with one hand leaning on her umbrella, turned a new and charming face to him, her eyes softened by tears and her mouth sad and tender. She gazed all round the room, taking in the muted green walls, the windows in which the orange-coloured daylight was dying, the Japanese robe that blazed in the shadow and said:

'I'm sorry to leave here. You can't know what a new feeling that is for me.'

Maugis nodded very gravely.

'I do know. I haven't done many decent things in my whole life. Leave me that flower for my buttonhole: your regret.'

With her hand on the door, she beseeched him, very low:

'What am I to do now?'

'Go back to Antoine.'

'And then?'

'And then ... *I* don't know ... long walks, sports, fresh air, charitable works ...'

'Sewing!'

'Oh, no, that ruins the fingers. Besides, there is also literature ...'

'And travel. Thanks. Good-bye.'

She held up her cheek to him, then hesitated for a moment, her lips half open.

'What is it, little one?'

She creased the pure arch of her fair eyebrows. She wanted to say: 'You're a surprise in my life, a welcome surprise, you slightly caustic, slightly comic, very sad man. You haven't given me the treasure that is my right and that I shall go on searching for, even in the mud, but you've distracted my thought from it. You've amazed me by teaching me that another love, different from passion, can flourish in the very shadow of passion. For you desire me, and you renounce me. So then something in me means more to you than my beauty?'

She shrugged her shoulders with a weary gesture, hoping that Maugis would understand all the uncertainty and weakness, and the gratitude too, that was expressed in the clasp of her little gloved hand. The heavy moustache brushed once more against her warm cheek and Minne was gone.

She almost ran. Not because she deigned to worry about the time or about Antoine. She ran because her state of mind required haste and movement. She hurried down the Avenue Wagram, surprised to find the air so blue after the yellow room. The Japanese lacquer-trees strewed the pavement with their withered catkins and the spring evening brought a touch of frost to the end of the mild day.

Suddenly she felt someone behind her, someone following her and catching up with her. She turned round and was not surprised to see the contemptible boy, who that day at the Palais de Glace, had not dared to . . .

All she said was: 'Ah!'

Jacques Couderc perfectly understood the intonation and meaning of that *Ah!* It meant: 'It's you? Again? By what right?' She stood facing him, straightforward and decisive, her hair less smooth than usual, one of her bare hands gathering up the long folds of her skirt.

He knew in advance it was hopeless. Not a word of pity would issue from that closed mouth and those black eyes, which reflected a pink glow from the setting sun, told him clearly to die, to die then and there, on the spot. He bowed his head and scraped the pavement with the tip of his walking-stick. He could feel her merciless eyes gauging how much thinner he had grown by how loosely his overcoat hung and how his trousers, too wide for him now, flapped round his ankles.

'Minne!'

'What?'

'I've been following you.'

'Obviously.'

'I know where you've come from.'

'Well?'

'I'm suffering appallingly, Minne, and I don't understand.'

'I'm not asking you to understand.'

The harshness of Minne's voice caused Jacques physical pain. He raised a face that looked like a tuberculous street-urchin's in supplication.

'Minne – don't you find me changed?'

'A bit peaky. You should go home: the night air's too chilly for you.'

He swallowed his saliva with a painful movement of his neck and his blood rushed up into his cheeks in a single spurt, restoring their youthful transparency.

'Minne . . . you exaggerate!'

'I beg your pardon?'

'You exaggerate your . . . your indifference to me! I must have some explanation.'

'No.'

'Yes. Here and now! You don't want to have anything more to do with me? You don't want to belong to me any more? You . . . you don't love me any more?'

She had let go the folds of her skirt and stood facing him, upright, with her arms by her sides and her fists clenched. Once again he saw that terrible, probing gaze travelling slowly up from his feet to his face, defying him.

'Answer!' he exclaimed very low.

'I don't love you. I loathe you – your body – the very memory of you – I loathe you!'

'Why?'

She threw out her arms and let them fall again in a gesture of ignorance.

'I don't know. I assure you I don't know why. There's something about you that infuriates me. The shape of your face, the sound of your voice, it's like . . . It's worse than insults. I wish I did know why, because, after all, it's strange when you come to think of it.'

She spoke with restraint, trying to find words that would mitigate her fierce, uncontrollable aversion and make her sound more human and understandable.

'Yet you can sleep with that old man!' he exclaimed savagely.

'What old man?'

'The old man whose flat you've just come from, that disgusting bald drunkard, that . . . that . . .'

Minne gave a peculiar laugh.

'Don't try to find any more adjectives,' she interrupted. 'That's another story you wouldn't understand in the least.'

She drew in a deep breath and her gaze left the face of the boy and lost itself in the wintry mauve sky.

'I find it difficult enough to understand it myself,' she said at last.

Jacques misunderstood her. He thought he was hearing her admit to a shameful, almost perverse passion and he clenched his teeth.

'I'll kill you,' he muttered.

She was thinking of other things, staring at the sky.

'Do you hear me, Minne?'

'Sorry . . . What were you saying?'

He felt a fool. One does not repeat such a threat, one executes it.

'I'll kill you,' he reiterated more feebly. 'And afterwards I'll kill myself.'

Minne's face lit up with a ferocious gaiety.

'Do it at once! Straight away! Kill yourself first! Vanish from my sight, go away, die! Why didn't you think of it sooner?'

He stared at her, open-mouthed. She was hurrying him towards death as if towards the inevitable end.

'You honestly want me to die? You honestly do?' he asked, strangely softened.

'Yes!' cried Minne with her whole heart. 'You love me, I don't love you. Isn't everything over for you? Isn't death the only hope of any life that love refuses to consummate?'

The boy whom she was dooming to death seemed on the very verge of understanding her and burst out:

'Ah Minne, that's true, that's true! After you, all other women . . .'

'There are no other women, if you love me!'

He repeated, like an echo:

'No, Minne, there are no other women.'

'One should not be able to change one's love, should one; whether that love brings you death or life? Isn't that true? Say so! Say so!'

162

'Yes, Minne.'

'Wait, tell me something else. You loved me, just like that, suddenly, without knowing what would happen to you, without foreseeing it? Yes? And doesn't love come like that, treacherously, at its own time? Doesn't it seize you when you think you're free, when you feel appallingly lonely and free?'

'Ah, yes,' he groaned.

'Wait! Love, I'm told, can come at any age. Tell me – you who love – can it come to cripples, to people born under a curse, to . . . to me myself?'

He inclined his head gravely.

'May some god hear you!' she breathed fervently. 'And, if you love me, leave me in peace – for ever!'

She ran off again, in the direction of the Avenue Villiers, feeling light and liberated. She went mechanically through the daily routine of crossing the vestibule, going up in the lift and sending it down again and ringing the doorbell. When the door opened, she found herself face to face with her husband. Antoine had been waiting for her.

'Where have you been?'

She blinked in the bright light and stared at him, startled.

'I've been shopping.'

She was breathing fast and her bare hands were fidgeting awkwardly with the knot of her veil. Her dark-ringed eyes wandered about with a lost, almost frightened look and when she took off her hat, it revealed a dishevelled mass of hastily pinned-up hair.

'Minne!' Antoine exclaimed in a thunderous voice.

She turned pale and threw up her arms to protect her face. The gesture revealed her badly-tied scarf. She put on such a charming expression of injured innocence that Antoine no longer had any doubts.

'Where have you been, I say?'

How large he looked, looming up dark against the bright light! His shoulders were hunched and heavy, like those of the Wild Man of the Woods.

'You won't tell me where you've been?'

Minne saw herself again, naked and chaste, on Maugis' knees. Her memory went back to the yellow and green room, to the sentimental rake who had not wanted her and had sent her away sad, happy and touched. A hand which had not caressed her breasts or her legs had dried her tears. The memory was both sweet and poignant; it had the fresh bitter taste of sea-water.

'You're laughing, you bitch! *I'll* give you something to laugh about!'

'I forbid you to speak to me in that tone!'

The scolding voice had wounded Minne. She recovered her normal hard, bold, lying self.

'You forbid me! You forbid me!'

'Precisely. I forbid you. I'm not a housemaid who's stayed out all night!'

'You're worse than that! I've had enough of . . .'

'If you've had enough, go away!'

She leant against the mantelpiece, her body rather limp, her hair dishevelled and her mouth drooping. All her defiance was concentrated in her splendid eyes, the obstinate defiance of a noble, angry little animal whose apparent weakness is only one more lie. Antoine pounded the back of a chair and snorted like a horse.

'Tell me where you've been!'

'I've been shopping.'

'You're lying.'

She shrugged her shoulders contemptuously.

'Why should I?'

'Where have you been, in the name of . . .'

'You bore me. I'm going to bed.'

'Take care, Minne.'

She raised her chin and said impertinently:

'Take care? My dear, I never do anything else!'

Antoine lowered his head and pointed his finger at the door.

'Go to your room! I know you won't give in and I don't want to give you hell before I know.'

She obeyed slowly, trailing her long skirt behind her. And, as he strained his ears, hoping he knew not what, he heard the key turn in the lock with a sharp click, like the click of a revolver being cocked.

Antoine, who had asked 'the boss' for an afternoon off, was striding up the Boulevard des Batignolles. He was looking for the Rue des Dames ... *Rue des Dames, Cabinet Camille.* Rue des Dames! The name struck Antoine as one of fate's ironies. His imagination pictured a vast organization, a police department for the investigation of feminine adultery, a thousand bloodhounds let loose in Paris on the track of as many erring little ladies.

117, Rue des Dames. The appearance of the building was against it. Guided by a smell of boiled cabbage, Antoine groped his way up to the concierge's lodge, perched on a half-way landing.

'Cabinet Camille, please?'

'Upstairs. Third floor, to the left.'

The spiral staircase wound up through a gloom that smelt of mildew. Antoine stumbled on its tiny low steps, not daring to touch the sticky handrail. On the third floor, a little daylight coming from a small courtyard enabled him to read, engraved on a tarnished brass plate, the words: *Cabinet Camille, Private Enquiries.* There was no bell, but a written notice asked the visitor to enter without knocking.

'Should I go in? What a filthy hole! Shall I come back another day? But the boss has only given me one afternoon.'

He made up his mind, turned the door-handle, and found himself once again in darkness. It smelt of onions and stale tobacco. He was about to turn on his heels and go when a violent voice from behind a door restrained him.

'You clumsy ass! Gone and messed it up again, eh? Messed it up again good and proper. Fancies himself a real expert in the art of shadowing, and then goes and loses her in a big shop! Why I'd be ashamed, *I* would, to admit I'd lost a client in a big shop! A child of seven could shadow a sewer-rat for you in a big shop!'

There was silence, then a confused muttering of a voice obviously making excuses.

'Yes, yes, go and tell all that to the cuckold. As for me, old boy, I'm fed to the teeth with your capers and if you want a kick in the arse . . .'

Antoine blushed and sweated in the gloom, with the absurd feeling that the 'cuckold' they were talking about in there was himself. Furiously, he knocked on the invisible door and, without waiting for an answer, entered.

The room was bare and damp; it looked clean at first sight, although a blue mist dimmed the mirror in the tarnished gilt frame. A shady-looking individual hastily shut an open drawer in which a long loaf, a large sausage wrapped in silver foil and an American police-truncheon lay side by side.

'What do you want, Sir?'

Antoine walked forward and stumbled over a long foot. The foot belonged to a pitiful creature sitting against the mantelpiece on a pile of green folders; a tall, bony creature who looked like an unfrocked priest and whose face was all lop-sided as if it had been bashed out of shape by the slanging he had just received.

'I wish to speak to Monsieur Camille.'

'That is who I am, Sir.'

Monsieur Camille bowed to Antoine with an easy condescension justified by the extremely French elegance of his get-up – plum coloured waistcoat with carved buttons, shawl-collared overcoat, stiff high collar and purple cravat with a horseshoe tie-pin.

'Sit down, Sir. What can I do for you?'

'The reason I have come to you, Monsieur Camille, is this. I want to get some information about a lady . . . I have no suspicions but, still, one likes to be well-informed, doesn't one?'

Monsieur Camille raised a pontifical hand adorned with two rings.

'It is the duty of every sensible man.'

Then he gave an indulgent, knowing nod and pinched his riding-master's moustache while his ruffianly eyes scrutinized Antoine, discovering in him the mug, the blessed mug.

'In a word, it concerns my wife. I am obliged to leave her alone all day and she is very young, easily influenced. In short, Monsieur Camille, I want you to let me know how my wife spends her day, hour by hour.'

'Nothing easier.'

'It would need someone very expert: she is suspicious, highly intelligent.'

Monsieur Camille smiled and put his thumbs in the pockets of his waistcoat.

'My dear sir, you couldn't have come at a better moment. I have someone absolutely reliable, one of those modest, unknown geniuses . . .'

'Aha!' said Antoine with interest.

With his chin, Monsieur Camille indicated the creature over by the mantelpiece who promptly hunched his shoulders in anticipation of the next dressing-down.

'What? Is that . . .'

'My best bloodhound, Sir. And now, if you're agreeable, we'll go into the question of fees.'

Antoine was too prostrated to go on listening. He would pay anything they liked . . . but without hope.

'Luck's against me,' he thought gloomily. 'That downtrodden idiot will never be capable of shadowing Minne. It's too bad to have gone and picked on a hole like this when there are hundreds of agencies which must surely be better . . . Everything's against me!'

As he descended the dark stairs that smelt of cabbage and urinals, he fancied he could still hear a furious voice shouting:

'And he goes and loses her for me in a big shop! Go and tell that to the cuckold and see if he swallows it!'

'I'd rather have been unhappy,' soliloquized Minne. 'People don't sufficiently realize that the absence of unhappiness makes one depressed. A good, sharp unhappiness, increased and renewed every hour is hell, all right! But it's a varied, stimulating, exciting hell that keeps you alive and puts some colour into life!'

She shook out her flowing hair over her white dressing-gown, and, unconsciously plagiarizing Mélisande, repeated: 'I am not happy here . . .'

Antoine had left home just now without asking if his wife were awake, but leaving a message that he would be out to lunch.

'Now there's a man,' she told herself, 'who's quite impossible to understand! As long as I deceived him he was perfectly contented. And then I dismiss Jacques Couderc, I send him to the devil – and then Maugis treats me like a little sister – whereupon Antoine becomes terrible!'

The truth was that Antoine, shattered at the idea that a spy was going to follow Minne all day, had fled. He imagined his Minne, his naughty Minne, held for hours on the end of an invisible thread, his gay and guilty Minne hurrying off to adultery, hailing a cab in her shrill, impatient voice without suspecting that, behind her, an eye was noting the time, the place and the number of the cab.

He had fled, after an abominable night, for his love revolted at these pictures and nearly drove him to take Minne's side and tell her: 'Don't go there! A horrible man is waiting to follow you!' He had fled, almost in tears, convinced that he had killed his happiness . . . 'They gave her to me to make her happy,' he pleaded on Minne's behalf.

'But she did not swear to find happiness through me.'

During that night he had wished for old age, for impotence, but not for death. He had considered a hundred possibilities but not that of a separation. He had foreseen a bitter and humiliating future, for the greatest love is that which consents to sharing the beloved. And each time that he had writhed on his hated bed saying: 'This cannot go on!' he had had to admit to himself that he could renounce everything except the possession of Minne.

At the very hour when Antoine was killing time in a dreary café, Minne left her home. She went out for the sake of going out, attracted by the sunshine and with no idea of going anywhere in particular.

In the sky, white clouds were sweeping across a faint blue sky. Minne raised her nose, over which her tulle veil stretched tight, towards the blue and walked down the avenue.

'Suppose I went and saw Maugis?' She stopped for a moment and then started off again. 'All right, then, I'll go and see Maugis.' She frowned. 'Who's stopping me? That's it, I'll go and see Maugis. If he isn't in . . . very well, I'll come back. I'll go and see Maugis.'

She turned sharply round to go back towards the Place Péreire and in doing so hit a gentleman, or rather a man, who was walking behind her, with her umbrella. She muttered 'sorry' in an irritated voice, for the man smelt of stale tobacco and sour beer.

She repeated, obstinately, thrusting her head forward: 'I'll go and see Maugis!' and did not stir a step.

'If I go there, Maugis will think I've only come *for that*.'

She remained standing there, unable to recognize the belated awakening of a feeling she had never known before and which troubled her: it was shame, which is perhaps only a sentimental scruple. She had frittered away her ignorant body, given it and then taken it back again. But she had never thought that the gift implied a moral lapse, and there was nothing more virginal than Minne's arrogant soul. She gave a discouraged shake of her head which at the same time refused a cab which was drawing up to the kerb. She retraced her steps and walked down again towards the Parc Monceau. 'I don't want anything, I don't know what to do. It's the sort of weather that makes you want to have someone to tease.'

She quickened her step, her head in the air and her gaze following a white cloud overhead, heedless of the fact that her gesture revealed, as if on purpose, the charming cleft in her chin and the moist lining of her upper lip.

A few steps in front of her, a man was walking. She vaguely recognized the colour of his clothes, the limp form, the long hair falling over a grubby collar. 'It's the man I hit just now with my umbrella.' In the Parc Monceau, she came to a halt and rested her eyes on the lawns which were a fresh, vivid pimento green, then walked on again, intrigued to find that the man was still behind her. He was rolling a cigarette, with an absent-minded air. He had a long nose, placed carelessly slightly askew in his face.

'He's had the cheek to follow me? He looks a thoroughly bad lot! A satyr, perhaps, or one of those creatures who pinch women's bottoms in crowds. We'll soon see!'

She started off again; the easy slope of the Avenue de Messine looked inviting and made her want to run down it, bowling a hoop. She lengthened her stride, happy to feel her blood drumming in her pink ears.

'What's that street there? Miromesnil? Let's take Miromesnil. The satyr? He's at his post. What a funny kind of satyr, so dim and dreary! Satyrs are usually bearded and savage, with cynical eyes and bits of straw or dead leaves in their hair.'

She stationed herself by a harness-maker's shop window, long enough to count all the collars bristling with badger's hair and studded with turquoises that fashion dictated for all well-bred dogs. The satyr, most patient of all satyrs, waited at a respectful distance and smoked his fourth cigarette. He barely slid a glance at her with his yellowish eyes. He even spat, after a loathsome hawking. He spat in the sight and hearing of all, and Minne's stomach turned over; she would have preferred no matter what outrage to her modesty to copious spitting. She turned her back on him in disgust and set off again. In the Faubourg Saint-Honoré a traffic jam separated them. She would have put her tongue out at him from the opposite pavement, but perhaps it needed only that to unleash the monster's erotic rage?

The monster, with one shoulder thrust forward and resting on one leg, was taking advantage of the halt to scribble something in a note-book, after having consulted his watch. That gesture was enough to show Minne her error: the satyr, the earthworm, the repulsive admirer was a base hireling!

'How could I have made such a mistake? It's Antoine who's having me followed! The clumsy, clumsy fool, the schoolboy! He'll never be anything else but a schoolboy! Oh, so you're paying someone to walk, are you? All right, I promise you he shall do plenty of walking!'

She walked on fast, jostling passers-by, feeling her legs as strong as a postman's.

'The Madeleine? . . . that's as good as anywhere else. And then the boulevards as far as the Bastille. Splendid! I'm the one who's leading the chase today.' She gave a cold, little smile, seeing, very far behind, a wretched, hunted Minne, limping along trailing a heelless red slipper.

'The Avenue de l'Opera? The Louvre? No, there are too many people about at this time.' She chose the Rue du Quatre-Septembre whose devastation appealed to her state of mind. It was all pitfalls, barricades, gaping holes, broken paving stones. An abyss opened up, filled with writhing lead snakes. One had to walk over planks and skirt trenches: the 'satyr' would have his work cut out.

In fact, she would have been sorry for him if his ugliness had not been of such a repulsive kind. He was red in the face now, his nose was shining and so many cigarettes must have made him thirsty.

'Poor man!' thought Minne. 'After all, it isn't his fault. Here's the Bourse: I feel like playing him the Rue Feydeau trick.'

The 'Rue Feydeau trick' was the innocent delight of Minne's first adultery. To meet her lover, the house surgeon, in his rooms, she used to go, veiled, into a house in the Place de la Bourse and leave by the Rue Feydeau. She had found this house with the double entrance far more exciting than the embraces of the tall, lecherous young man with the goatee beard. 'How long ago all that was!' sighed Minne. 'Ah, I'm getting old!'

Old dodge as it was, today the Rue Feydeau trick worked perfectly. In the Place de la Bourse, Minne entered the courtyard of No. 8 and, as she emerged into the Rue Feydeau, providentially found a taxi.

Lulled by the ticking of the meter, Minne stretched out her patent-leather shod feet, which had wandered so far, on the pull-down seat opposite her. She felt mildly mischievous, but no longer angry with Antoine. Victory had softened her heart and made her inclined to be magnanimous.

It was barely five o'clock when she got home to the Avenue Villiers. Minne thought she was going to be able to allow herself two whole hours relaxing in her dressing-room with her bare feet in her little undressed leather moccasins. But it was decreed that there was to be no *dolce far niente* in a pink-curtained room for Minne; Antoine had come home!

'What? You're here?'

'As you see.'

He, too, must have been wandering about for a long while, as could be guessed from the dust on his boots.

'Why aren't you at your office, Antoine?'

'If anyone asks you, tell them you don't know.'

Minne thought she must be dreaming. What! She had come home tired, but in a most amiable mood, amused at having shaken off the bloodhound, and here she was confronted with this rude bear!

'Like that, are you? All right, my dear. If you've got so much leisure why don't you use it to spy on me yourself?'

'To spy on . . .'

'Why, yes! I don't know who you go to but they're making

173

a fool of you, you know. What a staff! Honestly, this after-noon, I felt ashamed for you! A man who looked like a street beggar! All right, then, say it isn't true – tell me I'm crazy! Would you like me to give you my itinerary? You can com-pare it with your agent's reports!'

She recited in an insufferable high-pitched voice:

'Having left home about three, we crossed the Parc Monceau, walked down the Avenue de Messine, stood for awhile in the Rue de Miromesnil looking at dog-collars in a shop-window, followed the Faubourg Saint-Honoré as far as . . .'

'Minne!'

She was launched and she was not going to let him off a single crossroads. She counted on her fingers, rolled her eyes like an angry eaglet, insisted on the detail of the house with the double entrance and, without his knowing why, the jeal-ousy that was like a tight, painful cord round his heart sof-tened and relaxed. He gazed at Minne, no longer hearing her gabbling rage. He was slowly realizing, confronted with this feeble, furious child that he had been going to commit the fatal mistake of treating her as an enemy. She was alone in the world and she was his. His, even if she deceived him; his, even if she hated him; she had no resource, no refuge but himself. She had been his sister before being his wife and even in those days he would have given his life-blood for her. He owed her more than his blood now, because he had prom-ised to make her happy. A difficult task, for Minne was ca-pricious, often cruel. But there is no shame in suffering when it is the only means of making someone happy.

So let her follow freely the wayward path of her life! Let her ride for a fall, seek out dangerous pleasures: he would only stretch out his hands when she stumbled. He would remain prudently hidden, like mothers who follow their child's first steps, with their arms wide open and quivering like wings.

She had finished. She had excited herself still more in talk-ing. She had screamed goodness knows what phrases used by pedantic schoolgirls, histrionic appeals for liberty, childish cries of 'Now you've done it!' Two little tears on the end of her lashes glistened iridescently and she had exhausted all her spite. Antoine would gladly have taken her into his arms, all tears, and soothed her. But he felt that this was not yet the moment.

'Good Lord, Minne, who's asking you for all this?'

She lifted her head again, proudly, and ran a parched tongue over her lips.

'What? Who's asking me? Why, you of course! You, posing as a silent martyr, behaving like an outraged husband nobly controlling himself. Controlling what? What do you know? Haven't your police-spies provided all the information you need? They're so clever!'

'You're right, Minne, they're awfully stupid! But that's almost my excuse. I don't know them, I don't know how to use them. And I ought never to have used them.'

Minne's expression changed to one of defiant surprise. She stopped pulling strands out of the blue straw hat her destructive hands had been busy ruining.

'You forgive me, Minne?'

There was a cold suspicion in her sombre eyes, the suspicion of an animal to whom someone says: 'Come on out!' opening the door of its cage.

'Come now, Minne! Do I have to promise not to do it again?'

The reassuring, slightly forced, kindness of his bearded smile disquieted Minne, who did not understand. Why the spying and why the humble apology afterwards? She hesitantly held out a small, incredulous hand.

'You're frightfully annoying, Antoine, all the same!'

He drew Minne's arm a little towards him. Her elbow yielded but her shoulder resisted. Leaning tenderly towards her, he said:

'Listen, Minne, if you wanted . . .'

The twilight had come on swiftly and hid Minne's face from him.

'If I wanted what? You know I don't like promising.'

'You don't need to promise anything, darling.'

He went on talking in the dusk, like an elder, like a fatherly friend and Minne was humbled by a sudden recollection, at once sweet and distasteful: had not another hoarse, kindly voice, only a day or two ago, already half-opened the secret cell of loving and suffering in the depths of herself that she thought was so firmly locked? She felt herself suddenly weaken with weariness and leant against the familiar body of the tall man standing beside her.

'Listen, Minne ... Chaulieu wants to send me to Monte Carlo for a big advertising deal he wants to bring off with the directors of the Casino. I wasn't very keen on the idea at first but my boss at Pleyel's is willing to let me take my Easter holidays before Easter. So ... will you come with me to Monte Carlo for ten or twelve days?'

'To Monte Carlo? Me? Why?'

'If she refuses, oh God! if she refuses,' thought Antoine, 'it means that someone's keeping her here, it means all is lost for me ...'

'To give me great pleasure,' he said simply.

Minne thought of her empty days, of her savourless sins, of Maugis who did not want that, of little Couderc who did not know how, of those ones to come who had as yet no name and no face ...

'When do we leave, Antoine?'

He did not answer at once. He lifted up his head in the darkness, fighting against tears, against the desire to bell like a stag and fling himself at Minne's feet. She was not in love with anyone! She would come away with him, all alone with him! She would come!

'In five or six days. Can you be ready?'

'It's rather short notice. One has to dress up down there. Wait while I put on some light: one can't see a thing. You won't be horrid any more, Antoine?'

He held her against him for another minute in the dusk. With an arm round Minne's frail shoulders, without clasping her too tight, without imprisoning her, he renewed his silent vow of giving her happiness, of letting her take it where she would, of stealing it for her.

'*Dix-neuf, rouge, impair et passe.*'

'I've won another ten francs!' exclaimed Minne, enchanted. 'Why ever did you say one always loses at Monte Carlo? Antoine, I'm going to another table.'

'Why? Since you're winning at this one . . .'

'I don't know. It's fun to change. Meet me under the clock.'

Antoine followed her with his eyes, full of admiration for her rustling white dress, her slender waist, her golden hair and her pink crinoline-straw hat. 'She's enjoying herself, what a blessing!'

Minne, standing behind the croupier, apologized to him politely and pushed her coin on to the third dozen. The ball spun, slowed down and tottered.

'*Rien ne va plus!*'

Minne was gazing down at a garden of roses and irises below her, a monstrous hat which sheltered an invisible lady. 'What a hat! I bet she's a tart.'

'*Trente-six, pair et passe.*'

Minne had won another ten francs. She gathered up the three coins and almost at the same time as she, a fat German who had also staked on the third dozen leant forward to collect his winnings. But a sharp voice said from under the hanging garden:

'Excuse me! Kindly leave that pile alone!'

'*Verzeihung! Diese Einlage gehört mir!*'

Tit for tat, the lady retorted, in German this time:

'*Sie müssen nur auf ihr Spiel acht geben. Das Goldstück gehört mir . . . Lassen Sie mich in Ruhe!*'

The man was stupefied. His eyes called the honest

company to witness, but the honest company was far too occupied with its own affairs. Minne could not get over it either, for the lady in the hat, the lady who was sweeping up the coins with the authority conferred by a guilty conscience was none other than Irène Chaulieu.

'Why it's you, Irène!'

'Minne! Wasn't that the limit? That man with the beard trying to take *my* louis! Don't talk to me, dear, I'm trying my little system, a marvellous double!'

Irène's short hands were busy fingering gold twenty-franc pieces, piling up coins, pencilling notes. Her predatory nose was bent over a grubby account-book and her ill-gotten gains. Under the hat like a herbaceous border, her eyes summoned the gold, adored it, ravished it, and her conjurer's hands stripped the cloth.

'Isn't she marvellous?' whispered a voice in Minne's ear.

Suddenly feeling as shy as a newly-married bride, Minne recognized Maugis. So everyone was at Monte Carlo! She was so disconcerted at seeing the journalist that she did not know what to say. He mopped his brow and blinked under the harsh light of the chandelier. He seemed older to her than in Paris; there were grey threads in his moustache and deep melancholy wrinkles in his professional buffoon's face.

'Will you bet,' he said, 'that I can hear what you're thinking of me?'

'No,' she said warmly. 'I'm very pleased to see you.'

'Madame is very kind. And where's the noble spouse?'

'He's waiting for me under the clock.'

'Is this the first time you've been to Monte Carlo?'

'Yes. I feel quite lost, it's all so strange here. Don't you think one sees some interesting faces, Monsieur Maugis?'

'I was about to observe the same thing,' Maugis agreed deferentially.

Minne, who did not like being teased, twitched her shoulders pettishly.

'You mustn't laugh at me!' she pleaded.

'Laugh at you? It never entered my thoughts, my child!'

'What were you thinking of then?'

'I was thinking that, there on your temple, you've got one single gold, almost silver, stray hair that's drawing a question-mark in the air and I'm answering "Yes" to it at random.'

She laughed without enthusiasm and an embarrassing silence fell between them. Minne, tired of remaining standing, avoided looking at Maugis and they both thought silently of a room with yellow gauze curtains where words had come to them easily and sincerely and their thoughts had revealed themselves, naked as Minne herself. They had said everything they had to say to each other, there . . .

Sadly, they remained mute. They were listening, in the depths of themselves, to the musical twang of a very precious little thread breaking like a violin-string.

'I'm not funny tonight, my child, eh? Not amusing you at all, am I?'

She made a gesture of protest.

'I'm not gay when I'm amused. And I can be pleased without being amused. Believe' – she laid her gloved hand for a moment on Maugis' arm – 'believe that I'm your friend and that I've no other friend but you. It's an effort for me to say this but . . . you see, I'm so unused to friendship! Go back to the table now. I'm going.'

'Where are you off to?'

'To find Antoine. He's waiting for me under the clock.'

He did not insist. He moved away, after kissing the small, ungloved hand and Minne was left alone, amidst so many strangers, amidst the buzzing, studious silence of the gambling rooms.

She shivered, thinking of the bitter wind that was sweeping the Corniche tonight. By an unlucky chance, Minne and Antoine had arrived in Monaco at the very height of a dry storm, with particles of flint flying about under a leaden sky and the Mediterranean oyster grey.

Deep in her thoughts, Minne eventually reached Antoine, who had been waiting for her under the clock, and she left the Casino on his arm.

The wind had swept the sky clean and a mauve moon sailed in it. The motionless palm trees staked out the avenue at regular intervals, the creamy hotels and butter-coloured villas rivalled each other in whiteness. But all over this lay the beauty of the clear night, and in the wind, which was growing warmer, there was a breath of spring.

'It's almost as mild as in Paris,' sighed Antoine.

Driving back in the victoria drawn by two bony, but lively old nags, Minne felt chilly and leant against her husband's shoulder. The carriage mounted the steep road up to the Riviera-Palace at a brisk trot and suddenly the sea appeared, dark and pure. A silver net danced on it, surrounding a long spindle of mother-of-pearl light, like the pale belly of a fish.

'Oh! Do you see, Antoine?'

'I see, darling. Do you like this part of the world?'

'I don't like it, but I find it beautiful.'

'Why don't you like it?'

'I don't know. Perhaps it's the sea. I've never seen the sea before. All that endless water makes us seem so far away here – so much more alone than in other places.'

He dared not tighten his embrace round the loose white coat and felt shyer than a fiancé. Since the night of the locked door, he had lived with Minne as a brother, alternating between suspicion and remorse, fear and anger – and now he found himself marvelling at the thought that he had been Minne's husband, that he had behaved to her like a self-confident pasha, that he had possessed her without asking her: 'Do you want me?'

Those days were far away. Nevertheless Minne was there, against his arm, and the flinty dust, sparkling like frost, brought a little of her lemon verbena scent to his lips.

They were silent till they reached the far too large bedroom from which hygiene and fashion had banished hangings and upholstery. The curtainless windows, with their shutters open, shone as bare as those in an unfurnished room.

Still wearing her coat and her rose-trimmed hat, Minne went over to the window and gazed out at the luminous night. The gardens of the hotel hid Monte Carlo; there was nothing beyond a dark euonymus hedge but the moon and the sea.

Only three shades of colour, silver, grey and leaden blue, composed the cold splendour of the picture, and Minne sharpened her eyes to make out the delicate line, the subtle mysterious pencil-stroke far away where the sea touched the sky.

This clear night which awakened an unknown sensibility in Minne's recalcitrant heart echoed with all the noises of day. Distant music came up in gusts; whips cracked and wheels grated down below on the steep road.

Minne felt as if her soul were dissolving into shreds scattered over the sea, flying under the moon. She tried to collect her wandering thoughts but they turned into an anguished longing for a warm shelter that did not exist. Nowhere, wherever she had halted in her search, had she found Love seated by the fireside and the figure in her dream had no face. Ah, how grand and severely beautiful everything was tonight and how cruel to loneliness!

Frozen, Minne turned back to Antoine who was in his pyjamas, smoking. She was on the point of holding out her shivering hands to him, regal little hands whose palms did not know how to beg and which were held high, when they presented themselves to be kissed, with their fingers drooping like white foxglove bells.

He was smoking a cigarette and appeared indifferent. But something in his respectable swashbuckler's face had matured; something saddened that equine nose and hollowed those eyes like an amorous brigand's. 'So he's thinking then?' Minne surmised with astonishment. Never had she thought about him so much. She began to wish that he would speak and that the sound of his voice would at last break the spell of that dazzling darkness which invaded the whole room through the naked panes.

'Antoine . . .'

'Darling?'

'I'm cold.'

'You must go to bed.'

'Yes. Put the travelling-rug on my bed. How cold it is here!'

'The local inhabitants say it's quite exceptional. However, we can count on a magnificent day tomorrow. The wind's changing . . . you'll see how blue the sea is. We'll go up to La Turbie . . .'

His remarks became more and more commonplace at every stage of Minne's undressing. As she displayed herself to him more and more naked, her body seemed quite new to him in this strange bedroom. She hurried through the process, no more bothering about modesty than if she were undressing in front of a sister, disappeared into the bathroom and emerged again, shivering.

'Oh, this bed! The sheets are like ice.'

'Would you like . . .'

He was going to suggest the warmth of his big brown body but broke off short as if he had been about to say something indecent.

'Would you like me to ask for a hot water bottle?'

'Not worth the bother!' Minne exclaimed in a voice muffled under the sheet. 'But tuck me in tight . . . Pull up the counterpane . . . Turn the lampshade the other way . . . Thank you, Antoine . . . Good night, Antoine.'

He performed his tasks eagerly, happy, yet so sad that he could cry. As he forced himself to move deftly and silently round the bed, his heart swelled with dog-like gratitude.

'Good night, Antoine,' repeated Minne, sticking a pale, cold nose out of the bed.

'Good night, darling. Are you sleepy?'

'No.'

'Would you like me to turn out the light?'

'Not just yet. Talk to me. I think I'm a bit feverish. Sit down a minute.'

He obeyed, with his fond, awkward alacrity. Studying her face with anxious concern, he said:

'If you don't like it here, Minne, we could leave earlier; I can speed up my business.'

Minne hollowed out a place in the down pillow with the nape of her neck and arranged her hair round her face, burrowing into its warmth like a hen into straw.

'I'm not asking to leave earlier.'

'I thought you might be missing Paris, your house, your . . . your occupations, your . . .'

He had turned away his head as his voice changed in spite of himself. Minne scrutinized him through her hair.

'I haven't any occupations, Antoine.'

He made a prodigious effort to keep silent, but he went on:

'You might . . . love someone . . . miss . . . some man friend.'

'I haven't any men friends, Antoine.'

'Oh, you know, when I said that . . . it wasn't to scold you. I . . . I've been thinking that, this last month, I've been an idiot. When one falls in love, one doesn't do it on purpose, does one? I can no more stop you from loving someone than I can stop the earth from turning.'

At every word he seemed to be lifting mountains. His subtle, ardent thought clothed itself in the heaviest, most commonplace words and this painfully distressed him. It was agony not to be able to explain to Minne that he was making her the gift of his life, of his honour as a husband, of his devoted connivance. Not to be able to find anything to say to this frail child he had just tucked up in bed which would not hurt or arouse her defiance. And what was she going to reply? If only she did not cry – she was so nervous tonight! Running out of words, he swore to himself: 'I'm willing for her to make me a cuckold, but I can't bear to see her cry!' He was aware of the intensity with which the beautiful dark eyes were gazing at him through the tangled hair.

'I don't love anyone, Antoine.'

'Is that true?'

'It's true.'

He bowed his head, overcome at once with joy and bitterness. She had said: 'I don't love anyone,' but she had not said she loved him.

'You're being very sweet to me. I'm happy now. You're not angry with me any more?'

'Why should I be angry with you?'

'Because ... because of everything. At one moment I wanted to smash everything up ... but it wasn't because I loved you any less, quite the reverse! *You* couldn't understand that.'

'Why not?'

'They're the feelings of a man in love,' he said simply.

Minne put out a friendly little hand from the bed.

'But I love you very much too, I really do.'

'Do you?' he asked with a forced laugh. 'Then I wish you'd love me enough to ask me for anything that would give you pleasure, *anything,* you understand, even things one doesn't normally ask from a husband, and then that you should come to me afterwards and complain to me, as you did when you were little. "So-and-so's been horrid to me, Antoine: scold him or kill him" or whatever else it was you wanted.'

This time she had understood. She sat up in bed, not knowing how to release the sudden tenderness that wanted to dart out from herself to Antoine like a shining imprisoned snake. She turned very pale and stared at him, wide-eyed. Whatever kind of man was this cousin of hers?

Men had desired her, one to the point of wanting to kill her, the other to the point of delicately repulsing her. But not one of them had said to her: 'Be happy, I ask nothing for myself: I'll give you jewels, sweets, lovers ...'

What recompense could she make to that martyr waiting there in his pyjamas? Let him at least take what she had to give him, her obedient body, her soft, insensible mouth, her silky, Circassian slave's hair.

'Come into my bed, Antoine.'

Minne was sleeping the sleep of the utterly exhausted in the rosy dimness. Outside, whips cracked and wheels grated as they had at midnight and Italian mandolines vibrated below the terrace. But the wall of sleep separated Minne from the living world and only the nasal thrumming of the music insinuated itself into her dream and disturbed it with a buzzing of bees.

The sunny, benign dream dissolved and Minne returned to consciousness in a series of uneven spurts, like a diver leaving the bed of a marvellous ocean. She breathed deeply and hid her face in the crook of her arm, trying to recover the sweet darkness of sleep. But a slight, curious pain, with which her whole body throbbed like a harp, kept perpetually waking her.

Before opening her eyes, she realized she was naked under her hair; but unusual as this was, it was a mere detail, too trivial to matter. Something had happened last night ... whatever was it? She must wake up quickly and completely so as to remember it with all the more joy; it was that last night a miracle had succeeded in creating the real Minne!

She smiled vaguely, with an animal content, at the light that filtered through the window-shutters. 'The sun? So we've been asleep then? Yes, we've been asleep, and for ever so long. Antoine's gone out ... I don't dare go and look at the time. Luckily, we lunch late, we two.' She repeated 'we two' with the naïve satisfaction of a newly-married bride and fell back on the pillow among her dishevelled hair.

'Come into my bed, Antoine.' She had said that to him last night, convinced that she owed it him in fairness, like a prostitute who can only repay a man's love with her body. And the unhappy man, maddened that the reward should be so nearly a punishment, had flung himself into Minnie's outstretched arms.

At first he had only meant to hold her against him. He had embraced only her torso intoxicated almost to tears, to feel her so warm and scented, so small and supple, in his arms. But she nestled up to him with her whole body and clasped his feet with her smooth, cold ones. Weakening, he murmured 'No, no,' arching his back to get further away from her. But an audacious little hand touched his secretly and, with one bound, he was on her, pulling back the sheet.

She saw him looming above her as she had so often seen him before, faunlike and bearded, and smelt the familiar smell of amber and burnt wood that his tall brown body exhaled. But, tonight, Antoine had deserved more than she was able to give him. 'He must have me really properly tonight, he must be truly satisfied. To make his joy complete, I must imitate his own sighs and cries of pleasure ... I'll moan "Ah! Ah!" like Irène Chaulieu and try to think of something else.'

She slipped out of her long nightdress, offered her soft breasts to Antoine's hands and kisses and lay back, passive, on the pillow with the pure smile of a saint defying demons and torturers.

He was considerate with her, nevertheless, hardly shaking her with a slow, gentle, deep rhythm. She half-opened her eyes: those of Antoine, still master of himself, seemed to be seeking a Minne beyond herself. She remembered Irène Chaulieu's lessons and sighed. 'Ah! Ah!' like a fainting schoolgirl, then fell silent, ashamed. Absorbed, his eyebrows knotted in a harsh, voluptuous mask of Pan, Antoine prolonged his silent joy. 'Ah! Ah!' she said again, in spite of herself. For an increasing, almost unbearable anguish was tightening in her throat, like the choking back of sobs about to burst out.

A third time, she moaned, and Antoine stopped, troubled, for never before had Minne cried out. But his withdrawal did not cure Minne who was now trembling all over and turning her head from left to right, from right to left on the pillow like a child with meningitis. She clenched her fists, and Antoine could see the muscles of her delicate jaws standing out, tense.

He remained fearful, raised up on his wrists, not daring to take her again. She gave a low, angry groan, opened wild eyes and cried:

'Go on!'

For a paralysed moment he stayed fixed in the same position above her; then he invaded her with a controlled force, an acute curiosity, that was better than his own pleasure. His brain remained entirely lucid and in command of his body while she writhed like a mermaid, her eyes closed, her cheeks pale and her ears crimson. Now she clasped her hands and pressed them against her clenched mouth, as if seized with a childish despair. Now she panted, her mouth open, digging her nails fiercely into Antoine's arm. One of her feet, hanging out of the bed, suddenly jerked up and rested for a second on Antoine's brown thigh, making him shudder with delight.

At last she gazed up at him with a look he had never seen before and murmured 'Your Minne ... your Minne ... all yours ...' while at last he felt her happy body surge against him in waves.

Minne, sitting up in her crumpled bed, was overwhelmed with a tumultuous joy that burst up from the depths of herself. She no longer wanted anything, no longer regretted anything. Life presented itself before her, easy and sensual and commonplace as a beautiful girl. Antoine had worked this miracle. Minne listened for her husband's step, and yawned. She smiled, in the shadowy room, with a touch of contempt for the Minne of yesterday, that frigid child in quest of the impossible. There was no longer any impossible, there was no longer anything to search for, there was nothing to do but flower, to become rosy and happy, nourished only by the vanity of being a woman like other women. Antoine would soon be back. It was time to get up, to run towards the sun that pierced the shutters, order a cup of steaming, velvety chocolate. The day would pass lazily; Minne, hanging on Antoine's arm, would think of nothing – except of all the similar nights and days that lay ahead. Antoine was noble, Antoine was wonderful.

The door opened and a flood of golden light poured into the room.

'Antoine!'

'Minne, darling.'

They hugged each other; he fresh from the wind and the open air, she moist, and redolent of her amorous night.

'Darling, there's such a sun! It's summer. Get up, quick!'

She leapt out on to the carpet, ran over to the window, pulled back the shutters and stepped back, blinded.

'Oh, it's all blue!'

The sea lay perfectly calm, without a wrinkle on its velvety surface on which the sun lay like a silver plate. Minne, naked and dazzled, watched, in a ravished daze, the swaying of a pink geranium against the window. Had it grown in the night, that flower? And those red-tipped roses too? She had not seen them yesterday.

'Minne! I've got such news!'

She left the window and contemplated her husband. The miracle had touched him too, she thought, giving him a new, masculine assurance.

'Minne, you'd never guess! Maugis has just told me a fantastic story about Irène Chaulieu having a row with an Englishman about some business of pinching louis – quite a little scandal. So much so that she's had to take the train back to Paris!'

Minne wrapped herself in a loose dressing-gown and smiled at Antoine, thinking admiringly how handsome he was – so tall and so dark, with his Assyrian beard and his adventurous nose, like Henri Quatre's.

'And then here are the Paris papers. There's a bit here that's not funny... You know little Couderc?'

Oh yes, she certainly knew little Couderc... Poor boy... She pitied him from afar, loftily, with a memory that had become kindly again.

'Little Couderc? What's *he* done?'

'They found him in his flat with a bullet in his lung. He'd been cleaning his revolver.'

'Is he dead?'

'No, thank heaven! He'll pull through. But what a curious accident, all the same.'

'Poor boy!' she said aloud.

'Yes, it's bad luck.'

'Yes, it's bad luck,' thought Minne. 'He'll live, he'll become a gay little roué again. He'll live, he'll be cured, after the amputation of that beautiful wild love he ought to have died of. It's now that I feel sorry for him.'

'He had a lucky escape, that boy, eh Minne? Wasn't he rather in love with you, at one time? Come on, tell me! Just a little tiny bit?'

Minne, half-naked, rubbed her dishevelled head against Antoine's sleeve, with the gesture of a loving, tame animal. She yawned, and raised her eyes to her husband, eyes ringed with flattering dark circles and from which all the mystery had fled.

'Perhaps so ... I've forgotten, my darling.'

More About Penguins
and Pelicans

Penguinews, which appears every month, contains details of all the new books issued by Penguins as they are published. From time to time it is supplemented by the *Penguin Stock List* which includes around 5,000 titles.

A specimen copy of *Penguinews* will be sent to you free on request. Please write to Dept EP, Penguin Books Ltd, Harmondsworth, Middlesex, for your copy.

In the U.S.A.: For a complete list of books available from Penguins in the United States write to Dept CS, Penguin Books, 625 Madison Avenue, New York, New York 10022.

In Canada: For a complete list of books available from Penguins in Canada write to Penguin Books Canada Ltd, 2801 John Street, Markham, Ontario L3R 1B4.

Colette in Penguins

Claudine and Annie

Set against the ritualistic life of a fashionable
spa, and Bayreuth, the equally fashionable shrine
of Wagner, Annie's emancipation is described with
the observant precision for which Colette is famous.

Claudine in Paris

Claudine sets out to explore Paris and meets a
host of new friends and admirers, but it is she
herself, hesitantly moving towards maturity
and an overwhelming love, who imperiously
commands – and gets – our fascinated attention.

Claudine at School

Observant, impulsive, malicious, chastely sensual,
Claudine in her last year in a country school becomes
involved in an amazing succession of emotional
experiences.

Claudine Married

Claudine, after a few years of being happily
married to Renaud, a charming man-about-Paris
who 'has no authority except when he is making
love', meets honey-haired, ultra-feminine Rézi
and a bizarre triangle is formed.

Also published
The Other One
The Pure and the Impure
Gigi *and* The Cat
The Vagabond
My Apprenticeships *and* Music-hall Sidelights
Chéri *and* The Last of Chéri